"A BACKCOUNTRY SHAKESPEARE. . . .

The inhabitants of Daniel Woodrell's fiction often have a streak that's not just mean but savage; yet physical violence does not dominate his books. What does dominate is a seasoned fatalism. . . . Woodrell has tapped into a novelist's honesty, and lucky for us, he's remorseless that way."

—*Los Angeles Times*

PRAISE FOR DANIEL WOODRELL AND HIS CRITICALLY ACCLAIMED NOVELS

GIVE US A KISS

"Woodrell alternates between reaming the language with a dry corncob and a particularly skillful kind of literary cabinet-work. Tongue in cheek (and in most other orifices), he celebrates blood kin, home country, and hot sex in this rich, funny, head-shakingly original novel. Woodrell is a ladystinger of a writer."

—E. Annie Proulx, Pulitzer Prize–winning author of *The Shipping News*

"*Give Us a Kiss* is a keeper. . . . Woodrell's Ozarks are cut as cleanly as Flannery O'Connor's Georgia and pocked with characters just as volatile and proud and unpredictable."

—*Chicago Tribune*

"Daniel Woodrell can tell me a story any old time. . . . He knows the voices of his people, and he never sounds a false or condescending note. . . . One hell of a lot of fun."

—*The Washington Post Book World*

"Stunningly original. . . . Not since Steinbeck . . . has a writer captured the area's language, culture and heart as well as Daniel Woodrell in *Give Us a Kiss*."

—*The Virginian-Pilot*

The Ones You Do

"Another winner. . . . *The Ones You Do* is like Rice Krispies—the pages snap, crackle and pop. Woodrell's writing reminds me of the late, great John D. Macdonald, that kind of keen eye for the local detail, but he walks his own walk and talks his own talk. Don't be one of the ones who don't read him."

—Barry Gifford, author of *Wild at Heart*

"Characters as screwy and dangerous as any in Elmore Leonard, and a sense of pace and language that never warns you whether a scene or sentence will end in a burst of poetry or bullets."

—*Kirkus Reviews*

"Daniel Woodrell has the genius to make poetry of a holdup note."

—Lee K. Abbott

Muscle for the Wing

"Woodrell does for the Ozarks what Raymond Chandler did for Los Angeles or Elmore Leonard does for Florida."

—*Los Angeles Times*

"The colorful characters and piquant tongues in which they speak . . . really have us swooning. . . . All offer hot-breathed testimony to the human gumbo that boils in St. Bruno."

—*The New York Times Book Review*

"Gritty . . . packs a wallop."

—*San Diego Union*

"Taut . . . whiplash action!"

—*The Evening Post* (Charleston, SC)

Woe to Live On

"Woodrell joins Douglas C. Jones and the few others whose novels of western history are mainstream literature. . . . The violence is fast and understated and bawdy humor relieves the story's intensity."

—The Kansas City Star

"[A] fine novel. . . . Daniel Woodrell has captured the devastation of war and, more importantly, the twisting of men's minds in *Woe to Live On*."

—United Press International

"Woodrell shows a strong talent for pared-down, dark-edged storytelling—especially in fitfully compelling, atmospheric, violent setpieces."

—Kirkus Reviews

"[A] renegade Western . . . that celebrates the genre while bushwhacking its most cherished traditions. . . . [The novel's teenage narrator] Jake Roedel recites his tale of woe in an improbably rustic idiom, with a malignant humor and a hip sensibility that are wise beyond his years and way ahead of his times."

—Chicago Tribune

Under the Bright Lights

"Woodrell's debut harkens back to the film noir stuff of the 1940s. . . . tough and gritty—stylishly so, with snappy one-liners and convincing yet witty dialogue. . . . a delicate, sympathetic and convincing portrait of a down-and-out underworld and its sleazy, victimized inhabitants."

—San Jose Mercury News

"[A] harrowing climax. . . . gritty, savage, bleak and quite powerful."

—San Francisco Chronicle

"Very tasty stuff. . . . Woodrell has the gift. . . . an exhilarating writer."

—Philadelphia Daily News

Books by Daniel Woodrell

Under the Bright Lights
Woe to Live On
Muscle for the Wing
The Ones You Do
Give Us a Kiss

Available from POCKET BOOKS

GIVE US A KISS

A COUNTRY NOIR

DANIEL WOODRELL

POCKET BOOKS

New York   London   Toronto   Sydney   Tokyo   Singapore

This book is a work of fiction. Names, characters, places and incidents are products of the author's imagination or are used fictitiously. Any resemblance to actual events or locales or persons, living or dead, is entirely coincidental.

POCKET BOOKS, a division of Simon & Schuster Inc.
1230 Avenue of the Americas, New York, NY 10020

Copyright © 1996 by Daniel Woodrell

Published by arrangement with Henry Holt & Company, Inc.

All rights reserved, including the right to reproduce
this book or portions thereof in any form whatsoever.
For information address Henry Holt & Company, Inc.,
115 West 18th Street, New York, NY 10011

ISBN: 0-671-02503-1

First Pocket Books trade paperback printing August 1998

10 9 8 7 6 5 4 3 2 1

POCKET and colophon are registered trademarks of
Simon & Schuster Inc.

Cover design by Brigid Pearson

Cover photo by Jonnie Miles/Photonica

Printed in the U.S.A.

This novel is dedicated to three
ladies whose support made it happen:

Marian Wood, Ellen Levine,
and Deborah Sweet

And to the memory of
my father

Robert Lee Woodrell

And He saieth, "Let the trumpets and the
saxophones swing, man, swing!"
—from his jazzy eulogy

and grandfather

Pedro (Pee-drow) Daily

"Now, if a fella only knew . . ."
—from his lips, many times

"All we demanded was our right to twinkle."
—MARILYN MONROE

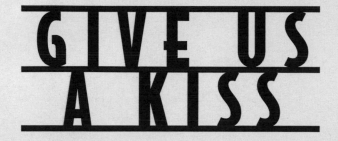

1

Three Finger Jerks

I had a family errand to run, that's all, but I decided to take a pistol. It was just a little black thirty-two ladystinger and I tucked it into the blue pillowcase that held my traveling clothes. The pillowcase sat on the passenger's seat, because you never know when you'll need to slide a hand in there, all of a sudden, somewhere along the road. I was on the drift back from California to someplace that didn't have any bench warrants out on me, and naturally I'd showed my face at my folks' place in K.C., and they saw I had the spare time to take on errands for them. There was no point in arguing. This errand I wanted to do anyway, pretty much, just to see the details of the situation and to note the conclusion, should there be one. After I tuned the radio to a station playing good cornpone driving tunes, I pointed the sort of stagnant pond–green Volvo with Missouri plates I was driving, which probably was on hot sheets as a yellow Volvo with California plates, into

1

traffic on Highway 71, and booked it south from Kansas City.

The law had come nosing around for Smoke again, and Mom and General Jo asked if I wouldn't go back down home, find my big brother, and talk some sense at him. The Kansas City law had a serious warrant, and, really, truth was on their side, but us Redmonds have never been the sort of bloodline who'll give our kin up easy to the penitentiary. It is one of our legends of our hillbilly selves, our heritage and genetic demeanor, that we don't truckle before authority. Mom and General Jo had squared up long ago and gotten a straight life going for themselves on the Kansas side of Kansas City near Thirty-ninth and Rainbow, but these cops on Smoke's case had lost patience with their recitations of ignorance and were getting all bent out of shape. Smoke was hid away down in the Ozark hills where we came from, and had been for over two years, but the folks figured it was time he came on in and tried to cop a plea. The law had been on their butts almost daily, with spot visits and surly phone calls at all hours, and had finally worn them out as parents.

"Doyle," General Jo had said, "you help us with Smoke, son, and we'll help you with your trouble. Your trouble ain't really much. Domestic shit, is all."

I'd said what I had to, which was, No sweat, I'll do it.

A hundred miles south or so I cut east and rolled into the Ozarks region, which is the perfect flip side to a metroplex. It's all meadows and hills, trees, and red, rocky dirt. The houses show signs of having been built by different generations with different notions of architecture, but all run together to make single rambling homes where the different wings appear almost to have been built

2

as refutations of previous wings. You start seeing chickens in the yards and huge gardens and swing chairs on porches and various vehicles that have rusted so successfully into the landscape as to appear indigenous. Quite a few weathered, tilting outhouses are still standing as a hedge against those fearful days when the septic tank backs up.

Our region, the Ozarks, was all carved by water. When the ice age shifted, the world was nothing but a flood. The runoff through the ages since had slashed valleys and ravines and dark hollows through the mountains. Caves of many sizes are abundant in the cliffs and hillsides, booger-gloomy tunnels that track deep beneath the dirt crust, toward the core, which is allegedly extreme in temperature. These mountains are among the oldest on the planet, worn down now to nubby, stubborn knobs. Ozark mountains seem to hunker instead of tower, and they are plenty rugged but without much of the majestic left in them. The hillsides and valleys sport vast acreages of hardwood and scrub oak and pine, with small, splendid creeks and rivers tracing the low spots. Here and there chunks of land have been cleared by that type of person who has no quit in them at all. Clearing a farm in this terrain often takes generations of bickering and blood blisters to get done, and these hillbillies stuck with it. As a reward for their diligence, they got to give a go at squeezing a living from chickens and hogs and stony fields of red, feckless dirt.

On passing such homesteads I think, Hats off to your hardworking dead and living!

Right near Green Eye I stopped at a Country Boy's and scooped a six of Busch and a couple packs of Lucky Strike straights. That helped a little. When I finally hit West

Table, Mo., our real home, twenty miles north of the Arkansas line in the bull's-eye heart of the Ozarks, the sun had climbed way up past straight and was evil hot. It might've been a nice day in early August if the heat was knocked down to ninety or so. The old boys sitting on benches around the square had their hats in their hands, fanning their faces, telling jokes that were fresh back when Bing Crosby's crooning made young girls wet their flour-sack panties. There was a kid with a stick stretching a softened wad of chewing gum off the curb, spinning a long gooey web around himself he wouldn't soon be shed of. This town, where I was born, and Mom and General Jo were born, and all of us on back past the Civil War were born, is still that way. There is a town square with shops and stores that haven't been strangled by Wal-Mart yet, with diagonal parking all the way around. The old kind of soda fountains still exist, two of them anyway, and everybody seems to know your face if not your name if you're a local Ozarker.

On the far side of the square I braked for two ladies from the bank to cross the street, their cotton skirts all clung up in their butts, by sweat, I imagine. They seemed to know the fine picture they made when they caught me smiling wider than just friendly, because one pinched her fingers up there and shook her skirt loose and less interesting, while the other fluttered her fingers at me and didn't bother. She smiled, too. I believe she was one of the McArdles, from three or four years behind me in school.

On past the square and down Grace Avenue I pulled in at Slager's Liquor Store. I hoped I could get in and get out without seeing anybody I'd have to jaw with. Everybody talks with everybody in West Table, and a ten-minute trip to the hardware store can yawn into an hour and a half of trading windy chat about hog prices, cousin Fannie's gout acting up, places where the fish are biting, and places old codgers used to go where, believe me, sonny, those Memphis gals did *not* bite. This is the surface of life here, anyway. Back behind the smiles and homespun manners and classic American hokum there's a whole nother side of life, a darker, semilawless, hillbilly side. The side of my homeland that has always attracted me, as it had all the Redmonds and Dawes from whom I spring, and held my respect.

Mr. Slager was behind the counter inside his booze store. He was a crisp little bantamweight fella, up in years, who affected neomilitary attire. His shirts always sported epaulettes, or else they were camouflage. You could get cheap thrills by sticking his spit-shined shoes under skirts and keeping your eyes on the toes. Slager was a decent old skin, yet he had a wistful air about him, standing in his store window in the uniform of the day, that gave me the feeling he thought he'd unfairly survived a patch of bad combat back on Pork Chop Hill or some battle of that vintage.

The store was air-conditioned down forty degrees from the outside, and it instantly chilled my sweat. As the heavy door shut behind me, Slager said, "Hiya."

"How're you, Mr. Slager?"

He didn't seem to know me, since I'd been gone quite a while.

"No kick comin'," he said, looking at me pretty close. "Whatta ya— Hey, you're one of ol' Panda's, uh, grand-kids, right?"

"Right. Doyle Redmond."

He leaned forward, as if to inspect my uniform, then snapped back to ramrod straight.

"My God," he said. "It is you—that ponytail threw me. And those whiskers—that's called a, what's that now? Goaty, eh?"

"It's sort of a goaty, sort of not," I said. "What I need is a bottle of Johnnie Walker Red."

"We got," Slager said. He spun around and reached up for the bottle, then about-faced and set it on the counter. "Scotch," he muttered. "Can't stand it myself."

"You have to work up to it," I said. "Once you get the taste for it, there's no goin' back."

"I've been told," he said. "I know ol' Panda prefers it— I didn't know you beatniks did."

I let that beatnik comment slide by, wondering if Slager had never bought a TV or anything, because that bongo-beatnik stuff was back about when I was born.

"What's the damage, Mr. Slager?"

"It's not cheap," he said. "Scotch. Too something or other for my taste. Nineteen dollars."

There was a poster behind the register that advertised beer while discouraging drunk driving, but it was the tall glass of beer that stood out, beckoned. A Bush-Quayle sticker was glued flat on the counter, and I put a twenty down on it out of the two hundred the folks had spotted me.

Slager scooped the bill, rang it up.

"Sellin' more and more of the stuff, though," he said.

"Now I'm back, keep it in stock."

"I do that for Panda already."

I picked up my change and the bag with the bottle in it, then headed toward the door.

"Take care."

"Give my best to Panda."

"I'll do her," I said, and by the time I was behind the wheel again Slager was staring off out the window, back on Pork Chop Hill or whatever, imagining himself dying gloriously with his heroic comrades instead of living on and on for no special reason except to feel semper fi and lonesome and guilty.

Panda's house was at the edge of town, just a few more blocks along Grace Avenue from Slager's, and it sat atop a steep nub of earth right up against the town cemetery, almost looming over the acres of dead. When I pulled into the pea-gravel drive I could see my grandpa the sportsman at the door of the side porch, a cigar in his mouth, a BB rifle in his hand. Since his knees went kaplooey this had gotten to be his hobby, hanging out the door, potshotting at the bevy of squirrels that run between the mighty, leafy oaks of the cemetery. The fact that there are plenty of squirrels still alive in there amongst the headstones gives testimony to how many years Panda has stacked behind him, because there was a time he didn't miss what he shot at. Once in a while he'll hit a car cutting through the cemetery and some poor sap'll come to the door to complain and get deluged with one of Panda's spectacular gushers of bullshit that usually ends when the fella with the dinged car apologizes and offers to drop off some tomatoes fresh from his garden. Panda is a pisser of an old man, and he's got a big mean streak and a big funny streak and fairly often they are the same streak. He delivers jokes that hurt and mean things that make you laugh, sometimes.

I grabbed the bottle out of the car and headed across the yard to the side porch, and Panda heard me and looked over. He dropped the butt of the BB rifle to the floor and worked his cigar over with his lips. His first words were: "Nice ponytail—reminds me of Liz Taylor in *National Velvet.*"

"Don't start off on me that way, Panda."

"It's the truth. Yours is maybe even nicer'n hers—more girly."

I held the bagged bottle up and said, "Got some Johnnie Red here."

Panda wore a white sleeveless T-shirt and khaki pants. He made a show of holding the door open for me.

"You're always welcome, Doyle," he said. His accent is deeper than mine, lush and basso, almost Delta-sounding. "Not as welcome as Johnnie Red, but more welcome than just any ol' hippie off the street."

"Blood bein' blood and all," I said. His hippie comment is twenty years out of date, and it makes me wonder what kind of time-warp conversations he and Slager must have, the one stuck on the space-time continuum back where a "goaty" meant beatnik, the other still seeing hippie-pansy teenage rebellion agitatin' behind the hairstyle of his thirty-five-year-old grandson. I just haven't felt like a haircut for a while, there's nothing else to my hairdo but that. Plus, nowadays every third Ozark timber-hauler has long hair and a beard, but Panda must see that as evidence that the ongoing Woodstock Revolution has him surrounded, I guess. He's a clean-shaven, flattop man himself.

I said, "Good to see you," as I sat at the kitchen table, hoping that what I said would prove to be true.

"Oh, sure—back at you," he said. He rooted his knobby hands in the cupboard above the sink, then came over with a couple of dusty glasses. His walk was unsyncopated, that big limp throwing the rhythm of his steps out of time. "Need ice?"

I'm trying to get along with him at this point, but I'm not sure there's a right answer to that question. Then it comes to me that ice'll be candy-assed in his lexicon of manly traits, so that's what I said, just blurted it, the Redmond love of petty friction coming out in me, too. "A couple of cubes would be good."

"That's how I take it," he said, outflanking me. He popped the freezer door open and snatched a blue tray of ice, then sat at the table across from me. The kitchen was dark and shadowy like the whole downstairs of Panda's house was—shades drawn against the eyes of neighbors, I suppose. All I could see of him, even at two feet, was his outline. He still made a stout, burly outline for a man with eight decades plus under his belt. His outline sat still for a bit, then his voice came from it, "Well, crack the seal, boy."

I pulled the bottle and busted the seal and started pouring Johnnie Red over ice, and it wasn't too many swallows before we were getting along just dandy, and I knew I loved the aged asshole inside that dark outline, no matter what.

By all accounts Panda was a better man as an old man than he'd ever been when younger. I couldn't've stood to know him, I don't think, when he was twenty-two or thirty or even forty, blood relative or not. His temperament was given an outlet for some years when he took up boxing, and from what I've been told he was a country-fair heavyweight. This was back in the days when a one-hundred-ninety-pounder was a big bruiser. Panda was a corn-circuit heavyweight during the tail end of the twenties and into the thirties. He tussled with Indian Jack Roberts in Tulsa, Bearcat Lee in Memphis, Cowboy Hussel in Omaha, Willie Perroni in Hot Springs, and Johnny Risko in Kansas City. Those fights were highlights. Most of his scraps were at small-town smokers and county fairs in places like Sedalia and Mountain Home and Joplin. He fought with a funny, crouching, cross-armed style he still liked to demonstrate, a style that by its odd tilt dictated he pretty much lived or died by the great left hook. In an era when white fighters tended to duck good black fighters, Panda didn't. He took on whoever wanted to tangle, but he generally spoke of this fact in a way that tended to strip the shine from his democratic gesture, "I always would fight a nigger in a minute." His actual record remains unknown, though he once told me he had thirty-five fights, with twenty-five wins, a half-dozen losses, and some no-decisions. He said he'd knocked out quite a few fellas but he hadn't counted them up. What has always made me wonder is, his lifelong sidekick, Jimmy Ware, who'd been both Panda's second and sparring partner, told me an odd thing I can't jibe with Panda's personality: this is, Panda's real record was more like forty or forty-two wins against seven losses and six no-decisions, and his kayo tally was over thirty. Modesty about his accomplishments is something I could never associate with the Panda I knew, who was not exactly a fella who underappraised himself. I think I saw him fight in one of my past lives, but

I dropped out of regression therapy without knowing if he'd kicked butt or been beat. My therapist was certain I'd bought a ringside ticket, at the very least. The truth of his record is there to be found, I suppose, in the yellowed sports pages of tank-town papers. I always planned to do the research and find out someday.

The thing that fits with Panda is, he didn't need to fight, he just enjoyed it so. When Panda came up, the Redmonds were still well-to-do, at least by Howl County standards. There are several pictures of Panda from that era, and he was always dressed more like a Kansas City boulevardier than a traveling country jake, which is what he was. He drove a new Ford to all his bouts, Jimmy Ware alongside him to fix his cuts and hold the spit bucket. I like to think of them back there in the heydays, tooling from town to town in a fresh-smelling Ford, nipping bootleg from a hip flask, two Ozark tuffies out in the world, having tumultuous adventures.

Panda's dad, Manfred, handed over the Redmond land to Panda a few years after he'd hung up the gloves and started staying put. The Redmond land in those times took a lot of minding, being over seventeen hundred acres of Ozark meadow and forest, acres that had been very profitable Redmond land since the year after the Civil War ground to a finish. Our land then began where the house still is, ran across what has become the newer part of the cemetery, clear over until it hit a little mud river called The Howl that marked the eastern border of all the fine land that was ours.

That land was ours right up until Panda lost his mind for a critical few seconds and shot some sorry wretch on the West Table town square. He did this shooting during a Saturday livestock sale, so there weren't more than seven or eight hundred eyewitnesses. This silly killing happened in 1950, not all that many years before I was born, and I think it has shaped my life, and General Jo's and Smoke's, too, in all kinds of ways that can't be proven but are sensed, felt, maybe only imagined. What would our lives have been like if we'd still been well-to-do instead of broke down to white trash and bristly about it?

The man Panda shot, three times, even once after the man was down and begging, was named Logan Dolly, and nobody says the man was anything other than a worthless piece of shit, but, still, that second and third shot were seen by all. When the sheriff, Carl Tucker in those days, hustled over to Panda, he said, "That first shot might've made you a hero—but you'll have to go down for the second and the third."

Panda's mom was still alive, and she couldn't tolerate the idea of her only surviving son doing life up in Jefferson City. She knew people. The Redmonds and all the kin hereabouts knew people, so the land, our land, and all our hogs and cattle and implements, were sold for less than they were worth, and the cash was ladled out to grease the wheels of justice. The money went to two lawyers, two judges, a state representative, a congressman, Sheriff Tucker, various key witnesses, and the family of the dead Dolly, who I imagine figured they'd gotten a damned fine price for Logan. Several weeks after the killing it was ruled self-defense, and Panda walked scot-free, and from then on wherever he walked people let him walk with plenty of elbow room.

I've never been told why he did it. No one, not even

Mom or General Jo, would answer my questions on the topic. I suspect that if the facts were let out, Panda's vicious act would look awful sorry, probably inexcusable.

But our whole legacy, a Redmond legacy that had taken generations to build, was burned up in bribes because of three finger jerks Panda couldn't control.

2

That Bullhead Looks Tasty

The bottle of Johnnie Red had gone a good ways south, and the sun was starting to slip down toward the rim of the world. I'd opened a few shades to let in some light, and Panda was standing by the sink, his feet rooted, but his upper body and arms were feinting and crouching and snapping short geriatric hooks at a badass phantom battler who'd had Panda's number back in the heydays. In regression therapy, which I fell into to appease my wife, it appeared for a while that in a former life I might actually have fought Panda, but then the veiled memories began to focus on a ticket in my former hand. Otherwise, this might've been me Panda dreamed of licking. He had gotten a good, sweaty octogenarian lather up. A chewy cigar chunk stuck out of his mouth like an on-off knob.

Suddenly he stops whipping up on the phantom who isn't me, and turns his drunk blue eyes my way.

"What kind of trouble you in?"

"No trouble at all."

"*No* trouble?"

"Not really, I don't think."

Panda assessed my comments for a minute, that stogie stub twitching rhythmically. Then he said, "That shit ain't goin' to flush, boy."

I sort of enjoyed being called boy. It made me feel like I had one hundred percent of my head hair again, and there was a long, rich life stretching before me instead of a promising future moldering behind me.

"That's my story," I said.

"You still married?"

"Legally," I said. "That's off-limits, Panda."

He put his hands up alongside his mouth and pressed his cheeks together to create a comic, woeful facial expression.

"Ohhh, l'amour, l'amour," he moaned in his notion of a pitiful Frenchman, then switched to what I imagine was an Italian immigrant, going, "Where da fore arta dou whanna I wanta you so a bad."

I rattled my glass of ice cubes and said, "Something along those lines."

Panda came to the table and dropped heavily to his chair.

"It's always along those lines," he said. He looked at the bottle and the ashtray full of Lucky butts. "We should be thinkin' about eatin'," he said, "and I know just what I want to fry."

"Okay. So tell me."

"Sweet, fat catfish."

"From the IGA, you mean?"

"Why, hell no. Sweet, fat catfish noodled fresh from The Howl, over here a ways."

"Boy howdy," I said, and laughed. "I saw this fish noodlin' trip comin' ever since you first said, 'Crack the seal, boy.'"

Panda couldn't walk it, so I had to drive. He sat in the passenger's seat, blackthorn cane between his legs, and shot scolding glances my way at any slight jostle, as if I was taking every bump in the road all wrong. If Panda's face was carved on the prow of a seagoing vessel, it'd be a vessel that didn't get fucked with much. He's got the nose job common among leather pushers, a honker carelessly crafted into a memorable, intimidating lump by six hundred stiff jabs he didn't slip. There's a little swayback an inch above the nostrils that rules out the strict usage of "flattened" as a description. Jimmy Ware did the best he could on the plentiful splits in Panda's skin, especially around the eyes, but his brows are yet cleaved by hairless puckers, and odd-shaped gashes have aged even odder on his cheeks and lips. He has the face of a man who early in life discovered pain and slow disfigurement as special delights, and never met the agony he didn't seek more of. But it's the overall glow of personality that gives his face that back-off-sucker sheen, as his smartness shows in his bright blue eyes, and along with the smarts obvious in those orbs, you can see the unabashedly mean and dauntless spirit of the man.

That is, he's a wonderful figure for a grandpa, by Redmond standards.

*   *   *

I took the route through the new wing of the cemetery, the dead laid out in democratic rows across a hillock and a swale where our hogs used to wallow. Then I pulled onto Jewel Road for a couple hundred yards until we came to the private drive of the newest owner of most of our land. He'd fenced everything in with pretty crisscrossed white lumber, and the only way to get to The Howl from this angle would be up the drive, then plow the Volvo across his immaculate grounds.

The house is a mansion built by drumsticks. It's a huge, impressive piece of architecture, even though Panda considered it just a boogered-up squatter's hovel. The notorious owner, Sam T. Byrum, sucked beaucoup lucre into his pockets when the red-meat scare came in the seventies and his poultry interests boomed. Byrum, or maybe his wife, Helene, had a deep-rooted fixation on *Gone With the Wind,* because this house is held up by the aristocratic white columns of the ol' Tara place the Yankees did wrong to in that flick. The power of film has resulted in this place, I guessed, and despite my atavistic allegiance to the land it sits on, the joint impressed me. There are white-bricked walls on either side of the drive, and though the gate was open I could see it carried brass-plated scrollwork that read TARARUM, a lazy mix of "Byrum" and "Tara."

I had the car stopped outside the drive, and, by golly, Panda's eyes had gotten misty.

"Go on in," he said.

"What?"

"Go on in, I told you." He stabbed that blackthorn cane on the floorboards a couple of times. "Drive on to The Howl."

This was the sort of moment, a key instance in fact, when Redmonds drift wide of the dully acceptable. The Volvo, I knew, didn't exactly belong to me, and was probably reported stolen, and there's an open bottle of Johnnie Red on the dash, and the blue pillowcase with a ladystinger in it is on the backseat, and this land hasn't been technically ours for near forty years. But we Redmonds haven't accrued our pungent family history by meekly toeing the mark the world has laid down, as we have our own Redmond world stuck between our ears by cherished myths and lies, facts and memories and inherited animosities.

Cut to: me naked in the Howl River, the brown water warm as spit. Panda had squatted on the hood of the Volvo to direct me, a novice noodler, on how to hand fish. There was an obvious wheel rut running from Tararum, past the swimming pool and the flower beds and the sexy statues, clean to where the Volvo sat.

"Don't be such a sissy," Panda said. "Run your hand up under the bank, into those mud holes. The cats sit in there when it's hotted up like today."

This mode of fishing, noodling, is a crime. The fine is around five hundred dollars, but Panda had a love for it as it was a skill country men of his age excelled at. I did not excel. I did not even enjoy it, running hands blind under logs and into mud holes—I am cursed by a bounty of imagination. Vivid possibilities rushed my brain while my hands slid into holes, such as creatures neither fish nor snake, but toothy and scaly carnivores that had lived for eons in mud holes and would soon snack on my succulent digits. All kinds of folktales about noodlers pulled under! by serpent-sized catfish and drowned (some of these stories are actually documented) or sliced like bacon by sharp fins, went boo! in my brain.

I'd gotten a two-pound bullhead by accident right quick, and I kept looking at it on the grassy bank, flopping at Panda's feet, thinking, That'll fry up to feed two.

"You're sloshin'," Panda yelled. "You won't get none that way, boy."

"I am not sloshin'."

"You been citified. You ain't worth a damn noodlin'."

He wanted a jumbo catfish, but, truly, I was happy with that bullhead. The sun was about to fade out, but there was a tangle of blowdown crushed against the bank I hadn't yet tried. So I slid that way, my feet sinking in mud. Just as I got there something came flitting out at thigh level, and brushed me like a cat in a dark room, but slimy and big, and all I could think of was a horrible thought about my privates dangling there like dough balls of bait, and I dove toward the middle and swam, thrashing hard.

As I clawed up the slick bank I said, "That bullhead is plenty."

Then I saw the sheriff, on foot, following our wheel ruts, with Mrs. Byrum behind him, standing back by the pool. Helene Byrum was a smashing blond lady, probably forty plus, but rich and sleek and distant. She was dressed in white finery, a wafer-thin and snug dress, very comely and chic, but her body language was clearly shouting, Get the fuck off *my* land, you white-trash goobers!

The sheriff was a tall, slender bullwhip of a fella, only a few grades older than me. He sported a big handlebar mustache he apparently doted on, pampered, as it was nigh perfect, and showed he was not only a handy fella with the tiny clippers and Butch Wax, but also fancied himself to be linked to the famously mustachioed frontier lawmen who had stood tall and firm and backshot so many white-trash bad boys and mixed-breed chicken snatchers while serving the public. That big official pistol slapped at his side as he came downhill. His name was Terence (never Terry) Lilley, and he was a butthole cousin to the Redmonds.

"Goddamn it, Panda," he said when he got close enough. His voice was thinner than he was, high and scratchy, but his face was stern. "You been warned to not come in here."

Panda gave him a straight stare.

"My mind, she is old, rattly," Panda said. "Things have melted out a here." He pushed a finger hard against his head. "Such as do this, don't do that."

"The lady is pissed," Terence said, then saw me come over the lip of the bank, naked. "And who is *this,* bare-assed and grinnin' like the wave atop a slop bucket?"

"Doyle," I said. "Redmond."

Terence nodded some, did a little fine-tuning of his handlebars.

"Oh, sure, Doyle, the little Redmond."

I'm six two in boots, haulin' two hundred pounds, but to many herebouts I am still Smoke's li'l bro. I stood there, shakin' water drops loose like a dog. I smelled strongly of Howl River, but that's a stink I never could hate. I started to pull my jeans on, and I noted that, up the hill, there, Helene hadn't looked away from me once, or gone into a high-toned, elegant swoon, either. In fact, she had a hand held above her eyes to clarify distant objects.

I cupped some fingers under my love works and made a show of whippin' river drops off. I made it appear to be a heavy job.

When I pulled my jeans up, her hand dropped.

Suddenly she was immensely likable, and the huge socioeconomic gulf between us seemed narrowed down to a mere crack that one good jump could carry me across.

Sheriff Lilley began to slowly amble around the Volvo, looking at its bad color in the fading light.

"Who did this paint job?"

"Oh, I forgot the name."

"Around here?"

"Kansas City."

"I'd sue," he said. He backed a few steps from the Volvo and the sad-assed paint job me and General Jo had done, trying to spray over yellow with blue. "I see paint jobs that a way when kids have stolt a car or something."

"I like it," I said. "It's different."

"It's real different," he said. Then he faced me and said, "You see Smoke, and I know you will, tell him to settle things with those Kansas cops. They've had a man down here twice, and they're pesterin' the hell out of me."

"If I see him, I'll tell him."

"Quit it—you'll see him. I've *seen* him a few times, and I could find him again if I gave two shits about what he done up in the city."

I imagine Sheriff Lilley's lack of resolve vis-à-vis Smoke traces back to us bein' butthole cousins. A butthole cousin is a cousin, sure enough, but it's such a distant, hard-to-trace blood mixin' that such relatives are called butthole cousins. It doesn't mean you're friends or swap Christmas cards or any of that, but it means you're kin of a sort, and kin of any sort means a little something in the Ozarks.

"You know," he said, "my wife fetched home one of your books, Doyle. She's a reader, I'm not, really. I never did finish it—too violent and silly."

I stood there and took it, this capsule review from a sheriff who'd once been the object of ridicule for spelling "law enforcement" as "law engorgement" on a campaign poster. I had learned to be calm before such philistines.

"And you," he said, whirling on Panda, "this is the last time I catch you trespassin' on Byrum land and don't ring you up. I mean it, Panda, goddamn it. You're an old man and all, but I'll ring your ass up good next time."

"I could do ninety days without changin' cigars," Panda said.

"Next time we'll see if that's so."

I picked the bullhead up, finger in the gills, which I guess I shouldn't have.

"And that fish is an illegal catch," Sheriff Lilley said. He came a little closer for a look at the bullhead. There was good eating on that bullhead, and it was still floppin' fresh. "I could ring you both for that right now, but I'm headed home." He held a beckoning hand toward me and I let him take the fish. "Now I'm gonna overlook your crimes if you get your asses out of here right now—'cause my, oh, my, that bullhead looks tasty."

3

Flame Licks

Whenever Smoke and me got together, something not too savory seemed to happen. In our teenage years we were like car wrecks that you knew would happen again, almost nightly, at the same old crossroads of Hormones and Liquor. I suppose I figured a little more age might have made us brothers less combustible companions, though I'm not sure it wasn't those dangerous possibilities that had me on this family errand at all.

The morning was hot by breakfast. There was a slight, hot breeze carrying the scent of the feedlot, which is a good stink, a stink cattlemen always say smells like money. There was lots of loot in the wind. Now and again, in the gustier moments, you could hear the beef bawling richly down in the pens.

I set out to find Smoke using Panda's directions. The drive would not be long, but it would take me into the countryside of our home territory, which is the same as going to church for me.

I was going slow down a rock road that had split away from Jewel Road, and the trees from both sides had joined branches above to make a secular cathedral of limb and leaf. When the rock road went into a low-water spot and I had forded a few inches of creek, I looked for the first dirt lane headed south.

There was, by happenstance, or nature's weird foreshadowing, I'll never know, a road-killed carcass at the first lane headed south. The carcass was hairy and stretched full-length, paws fully extended. It was a coyote, and its yellow fur was busted open in the rib cage area and alive with maggots, so that it seemed to be breathing, busted open or not. One of my past-life voices (the girl on ancient Crete who milked goats and was barren) broke through the veil and said, "Look closely, Imaru!" Imaru is what they all call me, even the more recently past ones. The exposed meat of the coyote showed signs of having been pecked and torn at by all manner of lesser creatures who would have fled before the beast when he lived. I guess I sensed the message but didn't rightly absorb it.

I drove slowly past the carcass and down the lane. The lane was only clear enough for one car to pass, and branches and weeds and stems beat against the Volvo, snapping and cracking encouragement to back up, get out of here. No voice guided me though, as they only come in tune enough to make out in a frustrating hit-or-miss style, like trying to dial in the Chicago blues station on the radio driving across Kansas at night. You might catch a few notes but you can't call the song, let alone the lyrics.

I bounced down the rut holes and bent back the

branches and pushed on. A house busted into view before too long. It was kind of an A-frame, but with double-A peaks, and a cedar deck, and an old yellow mobile home snug along the deck as an add-on. The deck was partly covered, and many a wind chime, all varieties, were hung from the roof. There were potted Norfolk pines about head-high growing near the porch rail, and a few peacocks and guinea hens and a couple of cats and a mutt looked at me as I pulled up.

The peacocks let rip with that wicked screeching they favor.

I got out, fired a Lucky, and sat on the hood. The mutt came over, wagging his tail low to the ground like a whisk broom, signaling in this manner of dog-lingo body language that he acknowledged my superiority and would enjoy being friends. He was longhaired, basically white, and spotted the color of an oil stain in the driveway. I petted him, and he grinned and jumped so I could reach behind his ears more easily. We were tight buddies in a matter of seconds.

Then the screen door slammed, and out came this vision of hillbillyette beauty. She held a pistol in her hand in a fairly neighborly and utterly charming fashion. Her long hair was a perfect champagne blond, and she had cutoff jeans on and a T-shirt that said COUNTRY BEAVER AND THE RHYTHM DRIFTERS. Sunglasses with a white frame hid her eyes. Her red cowgirl boots went up her bare legs like flame licks from hell.

She was studying me, a scholarly expression on her face. I couldn't quite speak, and she kept poring over me. Finally she sat the gun on the porch rail and said, "I know who you are." She slid her shades down her nose, and I saw for the first time her stunning green eyes, so smart, fearless, and ethereal. "I seen your picture on Smoke's books."

"Is that right?" I said, which wasn't much, but I was happy to hear myself speak.

"I've read 'em all," she said.

"Is that right?"

"Every one of 'em. Every word."

She was leaning on the rail, stretching like a fearless cat.

"Is that right?"

"You scared of me?" she asked.

"No, no. Just bein', I don't know—polite."

"Uh-huh. Well, you're Doyle, I know that." She came down the steps and over to me, her hand stuck out for a straight shake. "I'm Niagra," she said, and we shook. "Niagra Mattux, only Niagra is misspelled."

"Is that right?"

"There's an *a* missin'. Big Annie got it a li'l wrong on the birth notice."

She'd already said the right words to make a writer feel smitten, but then there was her, physically. I'd guess she was seventeen, though as I get older it's harder for me to judge. I suppose I was over-viewing her, physically, because she said, "See somethin' you like?"

"There ain't enough to them shorts," I said, "to wad a shotgun."

Niagra laughed and canted her hips so they flexed and became enchantments. Then she put her hands in her pockets and grinned.

"You act bashful, Doyle," she said. "I always thought you book writers were real pussy getters. Not so?"

"Sometimes," I said. This young girl was making a

horse's patoot out of me. "It's just those shorts, they're, you know, real, like, short."

"Uh-huh. Gettin' you hot or somethin'?"

"That's not my point."

"I think it is."

"All right. You got me, Niagra."

"I know," she said with a dramatic flip of her wrist. "And if I should ever want you, we'd be in business, wouldn't we?"

This kid made a heck of a first impression. She sashayed up the steps to the deck and said, "Want a beer?"

"Love one."

She went inside, came back with a couple of canned Stag beers, a brand you don't see in the places I'd been livin' in lately, but it was a brand I associated with being fourteen, out drinking with Smoke, barreling around in his '63 Dodge.

There were some wicker chairs, and I sat down on one, popped the beer, then realized it wasn't but about nine A.M. The beer was cold, and, though not special in terms of flavor, I sentimentally decided to love the taste and drain the nectar in one long pull like a teenaged rakehell.

The dog sat at my feet, tail swishing.

The peacocks cooled their screeching and went on about their peacock business.

Niagra curled herself into a chair, boots tucked up tight, and sipped at her beer. We sat that way for a while. I smoked a couple of Luckies and looked around. I saw they had a satellite dish rigged up on the other side of the mobile home. There was a barn down a pasture of scrub a ways, and a little pond.

After several minutes she said, "Smoke's not far. Big

Annie's with him, and they like to cavort in the yard. We should wait a while."

"Okay by me."

"They love to rut in the mornin', under the shade trees where the grass is all dewy and slick and stuff," she said. "You got a wife, don't you?"

"Legally," I said. "Not so's you'd notice."

"Hmm," she went, making a purr of it. "Another beer?"

"I might could drink another," I said.

She fetched it, I drank it, and she and me and the dog waited for my brother and her mama to be done rutting somewhere out there in the slick mornin' dew.

4

Spit Storm

It was edging toward noon, I imagine, before Big Annie came walking up from behind the barn. She was almost dressed. That is, she had a cotton print skirt on, the kind you wrap around and tie, but she carried her shirt in her hand. I had expected someone named Big Annie to possibly be a chunkette type, extra-weighted and all, but no. She stood pretty tall and had thick dark hair, but no way around it, she was called Big Annie because of those sizable tits, big melon tits that pulled down heavy on her chest.

When she saw me on the deck she turned her back and slid into her shirt. The shirt proclaimed that she preferred Dukakis in the upcoming presidential pissin' match. Then she came on up.

Niagra said, "Big Annie, this fella is Doyle, Smoke's brother."

"Welcome," she said, and by the outstretching of her

29

arms I knew she wanted me up for a hug, an instant
fellowship embrace. I am not by nature the instant fellowship sort, ready with a cheek kiss for strangers or the hearty
unearned hug. But this time I went along with it, and Big
Annie's hug was powerful. She must've stood five nine and
her arms were hard. "I'm Big Annie," she said.

"I see that," I said. "I'm Smoke's baby brother."

"We know," Niagra said. "The baby brother that
jumped grades in school and went to several colleges and
won't work for The Man, ever."

Big Annie slid into one of the wicker chairs. She looked
hard rode and put-up wet, but she had a smile, a blissful
expression. I came to learn that blissful was her norm, and
she had an in-tune-with-nature-and-the-cosmos sort of
constant sunbeam of personality. She'd been formed by
the hippie era and never found cause to remodel her
outlook or ways.

For me, I suppose it was the few beers I'd now had, or
the imminent reunion with Smoke, or the mention of
college, but I started flashing heavy on a robbery me and
Smoke had pulled when I was almost nineteen and only
freshly booted out of the Marines. It was one of the times
when the extreme measure seems like a lovely solution. I
was up in Kansas City, crashing with a sullen bunch of our
nation's naughty and wrongheaded young near Forty-first
and Campbell, more or less in Westport. This bunch had
developed crushes on needle drugs, but so far, despite my
susceptibility to varieties of self-abuse, I hadn't took to the
spike, though it came out of the shoe box and made the
rounds more and more. For the most part we were just
postponing the workaday phase of our lives from ever

starting. This bunch was about to pull me along into some fatalistic mischief when Smoke tracked me down.

Smoke fell by the pad with a plan. He'd had a union job at Kenworth Trucks, but they'd been out on strike for five months and, in fact, he was never recalled.

"Buy you lunch," he said, and we went to Mario's Deli and laid waste to some meatball sandwiches and marinated tomato salads.

After the meal, a delight to me since I'd been eating out of cans for a while, as none of the bunch I stayed with were into, like, cooking, we went down the street to Kelly's, where my being underage never came up, and dipped into a few bourbons with beer backs.

"I've got an extra pistol," Smoke said. In those days he wore his hair real neat, clipped short, and paid a lot of attention to his sporty attire. "And a plan."

His plan was pretty thin, on a simple level, and really all it amounted to was he knew who we should rob. Smoke had scouted the Git'N Quik convenience stores and discovered there was just this one cash collector for half a dozen stores. The stores were on the Kansas side of town, and, as I recall, my only comment was silly. "We should rob on the Missouri side, Smoke. That way if we get jumped up and sent down, why, we'll go to Jeff City, where Uncle Bill is. Uncle Bill could make it good for us there."

"That," Smoke said, "is a piss-poor way to think goin' in on a job. Banish it."

Anyway, it was coming up to Christmas when we grabbed the cash man over on Quivira Road. We worked naked, not wearing masks that passersby might spot and stare at. The cash man had a pistol but never got it out, as I believe he'd had a few Yuletide beverages. We'd approached him jollily, as if the spirit of the season was running full-throttle through us. The sky was gunmetal gray and ominous, but we got the man in the trunk, and it was all a lot easier than it should have been. Then the weather started, a twilight Kansas spit storm of sleet and snow. We were in a stolen car, naturally, and the streets were thick with Christmas shoppers, and before long the traction was slippy and slidy. We made our getaway on residential streets to Olathe, fleeing at about fourteen miles an hour, sailing on ice patches, the man in the trunk kicking at the lid.

I sweated horribly, I remember that, but Smoke was cool, maybe elated, as at ease in the middle of a crime as a brown trout in the White River.

We left the car in a strip mall parking lot and that was it. Fortunately the man in the trunk was heard and released before he froze, and he couldn't seem to describe us, neither. In fact, the *Star* wrote the deal up and gave our estimated heights and ages, but somehow we were translated as black dudes, black dudes who had gotten three times what we truly had, no matter how many times we counted it.

Smoke had seen I was getting too thick with that Westport bunch and pulled me out of it, so I could seek the education I desired. I declared residency at Mom and General Jo's for the in-state tuition. Then I took my cut, bought a white pickup truck, and headed west three hundred miles to Fort Hays Kansas State College for the winter semester. I had a GED from the Marines and a lifelong thirst for book learning, and now I had the tuition money, thanks to Smoke. Fort Hays was far from the city life and its myriad temptations, and they had varsity rodeo out there, and a fondness for red beer and books galore.

I dove right in to college life, and for quite a few years I stayed there, though at a variety of institutions, wallowing with relish in the sea of ideas and ideals and English Lit. and art history and studied poses, trying on different personalities, looking for a clean fit. Eventually I became who I am, a somewhat educated hillbilly who keeps his diction stunted down out of crippling allegiance to his roots.

All my scattershot erudition, so haphazard and difficult to find a use for—such as Ernest Hemingway (1899–1961) suffered night sweats from childhood, or pointillism is just painted dots that require distance for viewing—and my several onionskins of graduation, are owed to Smoke and his simple plan.

At the close of this revery of larceny and higher learning, I rose up from my wicker chair, Stag beer in hand, and said, "I need to find Smoke."

Niagra put her red boots to the deck and sort of poured herself into them until standing.

"Let's drive," she said. She set her can of beer next to the pistol that was still on the rail. The sun was emanating its meanest degrees of torture on all earthly items. "If you ain't got some bugaboo about it, I'd rather ride down in your car, though Smoke ain't far. A few big bumps and there you are."

5

Named for Trauma

The few big bumps Niagra guided me over beat my wife's not-nearly-paid-for Volvo down in value a good deal more, as I oversteered some, clipped a stump, grazed a boulder, bottomed out in a gully once. It was not far in distance but a punishing drive, from the car's perspective.

We were down past the barn, under a thickness of trees that I could see broke open shortly and gave way to a pasture gone white in the heat.

"Stop there," Niagra said. She had her boots on the dash to brace herself. "Whoa, Nelly."

We got out and stood in the heavy shade, and it took a bit for my eyes to adjust before I saw Smoke's hideout. A fifteen-foot trailer had been shoved up cozy against a couple of trees and rested on tires gone flat. It was cell-house gray in color, a color that I personally shun. A couple of metal chairs, the kind that rock, sat on the bare dirt in front of the trailer. Rust had attacked them pretty thoroughly. Busch beer cans were scattered around like strange blue blooms. The door was screened, and cordwood was stacked low around the gap between trailer and earth.

"Nice," I said.

"Well, hard to find," Niagra said.

When you're a boy you think someday you want to live like this. A little hole in the woods, your living space like a cave or a fort. The woods right up to your bedroom window, a rifle by the door in case supper strolls along and is standing in the yard when you wake. Women housed separately, nearby but up the road. Smoke's hideout would've met the standards of Thoreau, I imagine, if Thoreau had drunk a lot of canned beer and laid off of the heavy reading and philosophical inquiries in favor of ruttin' with Big Annie of a mornin'.

Smoke came walking in from the woods behind the trailer, a roll of shit paper in one hand. We saw each other simultaneously. He let out a big, throaty bellow and charged toward me. He wore blue-jean shorts and white tennies.

I knew what was coming. I braced for the assault of genuine masculine affection.

"Doyle, my baby bro," he said, and flung the shit paper toward the door. Then I was in the huge embrace, the rough hugs of my big brother, who squeezed me up off my feet and thumped my back with big fists of love. I did some back, with less effect.

He still had me in that big, rib-shakin' hug, when I said, "Smoke, man, what you been up to?"

He let go of me then, smiling hugely.

"Let's see, Doyle. I wrestled the devil down and fucked him in the ass. Other'n that, the same ol' same ol'."

I hadn't seen him in three years. Life on the lam seemed to agree with him. He's always been monster big, but up in K.C. he'd gone to fat for a while, but now, living in hard communion with nature, he was firm and fit and mud brown. He stood about six five, and I'd guess he didn't weigh over two forty or two fifty. Sleek. Smoke had spent his entire lifetime in mad pursuit of the elementary pleasures and his face showed it, with laugh crinkles all around his hungry brown eyes and a slanting pool-cue scar on his forehead he'd acquired from a husband who didn't appreciate Smoke's joie de vivre. Smoke always was the breed of boy and man who after he'd opened a bottle of whisky would throw the cap away. His hair was shoulder length, laced with gray, and somebody, Big Annie I found, had attended to his locks. They were braided in thin ropy strands, sort of hillbilly dreadlocks. His beard was perfectly groomed and streaked with gray, like tines in a pitchfork.

"You're lookin' good," I said.

"You too, baby," he said, then grabbed my ponytail and said, "Yee-hah!"

"Whatever," I said.

He let go, looked fondly at Niagra, and said to her, "You're gonna like Doyle—he's overeducated and starry-eyed, too."

She shrugged, considering it.

"It could happen," she said. "I've been known to like people now and then." She started walking off toward the house. "I'll let you brothers be with your re-union. But don't draw blood out of happiness or anything."

I dropped into a rusty chair and watched Niagra walk. Smoke did likewise. It was a walk worth watching. There was a slithery élan to Niagra's movements, as in the old blues phrase, "Like her back ain't got no bone." When she had gotten out of earshot, I said, "Is she legal?"

"Legal, hell," Smoke said, "she's an old maid. Turned nineteen last month. Got a year of JUCO under her belt at the extension college in town."

"Got a man, does she?"

"Nope."

"I can't believe that."

"Well, she's got her some strange ways and standards that rule out damn near every buck in the Ozarks."

"I see," I said. "Strange ways, huh?"

"Yeah. But you might get in there—she thinks you're brilliant. Read your books like they were love letters."

"No shit," I said, and my mouth filled with saliva, and I swallowed rather than spit so soon after hearing such an enchanting review of my efforts.

"But enough about poozle," Smoke said. "How's about a stick of boo and a drink? I don't have ice here, but I got a bottle."

"Hold off on the boo and booze, Smoke. We need to talk, so let's do it now and be done with it."

"Say it," he said.

I leaned forward, elbows to knees.

"I'm on a secret mission from the folks."

"Uh-huh."

"I accepted this mission for reasons of my own."

"Yeah?"

"They want you to turn yourself in."

"It's come to that, huh?"

"They want you to try'n plead out some sort of deal."

"Uh-huh."

"They've been leaned on pretty heavy up there."

"I know." Smoke stroked at his facial hair, his splayed fingers neatly matched to the pitchfork tines in his beard. "Let me think a bit," he said. Then, in about four seconds, "Okay, I gave it full consideration."

"And?"

"Ain't gonna be no days like that. Smoke don't figure to turn himself in just yet."

I got up, fetched the ladystinger from the car, and assumed a gun-totin' pose.

"General Jo sent this pistol with me," I said. "I'm supposed to do whatever it takes. So"—I waved the gun his way—"Freeze, Bubba!"

Smoke laughed, then said, "He sent *that* pistol? A li'l ol' flesh-wounder?"

"I don't think he trusts me with his strong armaments."

"That figures. A man that don't trust his grown son to drive his car sure ain't gonna trust that same son with strong armaments. He's a smart ol' man, you know," Smoke said. "But I got plans that require my presence on this side of the jailhouse bars. So I reckon that wraps that up."

I sat back down and relaxed, letting the ladystinger dangle. My eyes stuck on Smoke's wide, hairless chest, hairless because it was one huge burn scar, the proud flesh thick like a hide, from his nipples to his belly button. That's how he got nicknamed Smoke, because as a boy he really loved that bacon. Mom was walking the hot black skillet of bacon toward the table one morning, and Smoke couldn't wait, leaped up and grabbed the skillet side and doused himself with bubblin' grease. He was near six, I think, I was about two. I believe I recall his cries, or maybe not. After that, "Smoke" was tagged on him as a name, which he doesn't seem to mind. And me? I don't know. We've all had our traumas, but I wouldn't care to be named for any of them.

"Okey-doke," I said. "I tried. Gave it my best effort. Let's have at that bottle and boo now, big bro."

6

Cow Pattie Links

Later we were out in the bone-white pasture, trying to get in a good eighteen holes of golf on the cow-pattie links Smoke had designed. Everything was a short-iron shot, and the white weeds created a rough the PGA boys wouldn't go into on a John Deere tractor. The heat was there, of course, and seed ticks and cuff stickers attached to our socks and shorts and legs. Smoke only had two clubs, both nine irons, but he had a grocery sack of nicked balls and we both had the boozy imagination to see this activity as fun.

"How'd you like to find the path to financial security?" Smoke intoned, sounding somewhat similar to the mellifluous voice of golf on CBS Sports. He then smacked his orange golf ball, and we watched it fly across the deep white rough toward the stack of dried cow patties he called The Ninth Hole. He landed the ball pattie-high but left, not nearly in the turd. "Not rich rich," he went on, "but

40

rich enough to sit down and whip out any book you want
and not give a fuck if the public buys it."

There was a bottle of ordinary scotch, King's Deluxe or
something, set on the ground to mark the tee-off spot. I
gripped my nine iron and took my stance. I wanted to
win, you know. I hunched down, then straightened up,
shuffled my feet for the perfect alignment.

"You mean a grant?" I asked.

"I mean a hillbilly endowment toward the support of
artsy bullshit. Only without the bureaucracy and red
tape."

I had my swing grooved, and let her rip. I took a mean
divot but the ball really soared, way high, the kind that
makes a soft landing.

"Who do I have to kill?" I asked.

The ball flew directly on line, but came up short of the
turd stack and sank from sight in the white rough.

"Maybe nobody," Smoke said. He crouched to the
bottle of King's Deluxe, had a gulp. "Course, you never
do know."

Listen, here's the deal with me. I've got just one true
love, and that's the art of following my fantasies out and
scribblin' them down. I tell stories, yarns, tiny snickering
contes, big wet whoppers; only eventually, nearly against
my will, they shade toward truth.

My imagination is always skulking about in a wrong
place, a bad neighborhood of fantasy. Everything in there
takes place on Twelfth Street, U.S.A., and of course there
are joints and dives called The Pink Pussycat, The Aces
High, or Joe's, and fellas named Buster or Jake or Gyp the
Blood agitate the area, and rain murmurs along in the
gutter, clogged with trash but reflecting the neon lights.

Who hasn't been there? The hero I chronicle is not much of a hero, but he's given up four books to me. He's a little bit of a sleaze, really, but he hangs in there and pays his own way. He's called merely The Hyena, no other name required, and that's because he always gets a bite of the meat. What he does is float around Twelfth Street, U.S.A., where the interesting vices and poorly plotted crimes tend to be centered, and sniffs out deals going down. He stalks, trails, sniffs, watches. After a deal is done and the folks with the Twelfth Street, U.S.A., names and attitudes have culled out a carcass of ill-gotten gains, why The Hyena moves in to rip them off and eat all the pie himself. The Hyena is not too noble, but he's robust and goal-oriented and thinks of his deeds as butthole cousins to justice.

My books sound like I'm someone else, someone of much more age who hails from a time zone that's gone out of business. The Hyena talks like an old fart Panda's age might've talked if he'd been a rough cob in the city when the Big Crash came. The Hyena's approach could've been in favor among the Populists in 1932 or along in there. He's always describing people as "gunsel" or "jackroller" or "thrush," and he lips off to anybody with over three bucks to his name or a badge.

I always get called a crime writer, though to me they are slice-of-life dramas. They remind me of my family and friends, actually. I hate to think I've led a "genre" life, but that seems to be the category I'm boxed in.

It's hard not to like The Hyena, or anyway, I do.

"Hey, bro," Smoke said, giving me a shove. "Find your ball, huh?"

"I saw it land," I said, but I wondered if the dead voices

from past lives were ever-so-faintly trying to hector me toward sound judgments, or taunt me toward bold action.

I didn't ask Smoke just how I might get this hillbilly endowment for artsy bullshit, steered clear of the leading question, and he let the subject drop while we got in our sweaty eighteen holes of golf.

The score was close, one forty-seven to one forty-five, not bad scores given the conditions of the fairways and the tough course design, me nipping Smoke because of a tee-shot at the seventeenth cow pattie that actually hit the stack of turds, and busted them apart. I want to say they busted apart as do dried-up dreams, or public trust, but, truly, they flew apart exactly like yesterday's shit.

7

That Smell

Supper materialized and was a shocking and wonderful feedbag to strap on, but, by the time the classic hippie dessert of quartered raw apples and honey in a bowl came out, I felt there was a conspiracy afoot all around me. Smoke huddled with Big Annie, then Niagra, then all of them made trips inside the house and I could hear that they were whispering and so forth. I couldn't pick up any words or phrases, but I didn't need any hot flashes for Imaru to imagine the subject.

We'd dined on the cedar deck at dusk. Finally the day had gotten cool enough to comfortably eat in. I'd napped in Smoke's shady yard and come to feeling pretty sober and rested and mighty interested in food. The meal was Niagra's creation. She'd cooked up the first of her hillbilly-ette surprises for me: pesto sauce over homemade pasta, with a lovely salad of garden tomatoes and cucumber slices in olive oil, with fresh basil seasoning and goat cheese slivers. This marked her as a bookworm, a trait I dig in anyone, for clearly Niagra had done a useful gob of reading in at least the cookbook section of the West Table Library, because the nearest place to have learned this sort of culinary preparation by taste-testing it would've been Memphis, probably, or maybe Little Rock. The classic hippie dessert was served for the convenience of its preparation, I imagine, and was perfectly groovy, but by then, in my goggled state, I'd sort of been expecting tiramisú, maybe, or a scoop of spumoni.

As full dark settled I was left alone at the table while another big confab occurred somewhere in the house. I lit a Lucky and sat there, petting the dog. The dog it turned out was a spayed bitch, the best kind of dog for a pet, I think, and was named Damned Spot because Niagra had played Lady Macbeth in high school and cherished the "Out, damned spot" speech. I was the new "big one" in her midst, and Damned Spot had decided to love me into the pack immediately. I smoked and rubbed her, and plucked a few fat ticks from behind her ears. I put the bulbous blood ticks on the table, belly up, and dispatched them with the hot end of the Lucky.

In the dark, there, I started talking to Damned Spot. I slung all kinds of folderol her way, mostly about romance gone sour and along in that vein, and I was glad to have the dog there to say it to. A dog that listens is so handy to validate that, though you're having a conversation with no human present, you *are* talking to a dog, which is next best and means you aren't touched in the head. A person alone talking to a dog seems sort of cute, capable of tenderness and so forth, whereas if you sat there having the same exact conversation without a dog present to ameliorate the wackiness, people would quit making eye contact with you, call your mother suggesting mental health facilities. The dog makes all the difference.

When the confab broke up and the whispering trio returned, they were intent on business. They stood over me, executives lined together as a united front, the kitchen light behind them casting their forms in ominous relief.

Smoke said, "We need to know if you're in or you're out."

"In or out of what?"

They all copped squats then around the table. They took turns talking, a microdemocracy at work, but Smoke's words and Niagra's presence heaved the most weight. The long and the short of it was pretty much what I'd imagined it might be: wacky backy croppin'. Smoke knew I'd had some considerable truck with that product in years past, moved a bit of herb in the vicinity of various campuses, and also worked harvest two seasons when I was in grad school at Iowa and strapped for mad money.

Eventually I asked, "What might my share be?"

"You're comin' in late," Smoke said. "But we need extra security now."

"Why is that?"

"Some Dollys have been sniffin' around," Big Annie said. Dollys sniffing around is about the worst news a person could get in the Howl County area. They are a legendary clan for thievery and nasty shenanigans, legion in number, taking over three columns in the West Table phone book. "A bunch that runs with an awful man named Springer, who might be a Dolly by intermarriage."

"They're not as far advanced beyond the caveman as most of us are," Niagra said. "Rip artists. Not nice."

46

GIVE US A KISS

"Springer," Smoke said, "is a bad, bad man—he'd be good research for you to know."

I lit a Lucky.

"This would all be good research," I said.

"We act friendly to them," Niagra said, "but we're not."

"They'll burn you on a deal," Smoke said, "then dare you to come on and kill them."

"I reckon I'd snub a bunch like that," I said. I was thinking that this might be *too much* research of first-hand quality, though the quest for verisimilitude had previously provided me with an artistic alibi for many vices and scandalous companions. "Keep my distance."

"Springer'll shoot quick, too," Smoke said. "I'm pretty sure he killed a dude down in Viola there, across the Arkansas line. And I saw him shoot Bond Collins in the leg outside The Inca Club."

"Well," I said, "*him* I've just got to know."

"And your share," Niagra said, "should be right at fifteen thousand dollars, tax free."

"Assuming I live to cash in."

Fifteen K is more than my agent had ever managed to get me for an entire novel, including paperback and foreign rights, after his big bite of the capital was factored in. And this would resemble a lump-sum payment for a book I wouldn't even have to create, not write a lick. It amounted to a literary grant I could get without having to shtup three of the five judges.

I smoked for a moment, posed thoughtfully, as if in deep and detailed consideration of the proposal. The peacocks were up in the tall limbs to roost, not letting out much with the cackles and screams that are so ghostly when coming from high up in a dark tree, quietly on the alert for night-stalking owls that might swoop by and snatch their heads off. Damned Spot was on the deck, belly to the stars, shimmying her back against the cedarwood, harassing her fleas. The wind chimes tinkled as air puffed by, sounding like spare change rattling in the pockets of fleeing suspects. I wanted to salve my good sense by acting reluctant to accede to my genetic and family-of-origin inevitabilities. The matter of sheer personal choice intrudes and weighs in kind of heavy, too, I suppose, but to cop to personal choice would undermine my sense of deterministic doom.

I believed a message was coming in for Imaru at this moment, but it faded and instead I had a memory of or intuition about our daddy, General Jo, and his brother Bill. They were adults when the Redmond land was lost because of Panda's weak management of his emotions. Dad was named General Jo after General Jo Shelby of the Missouri Confederate Cavalry. Shelby was the only general in all the Confederate states who never did surrender. He and his Missouri boys buried their battle flag in the mud of the Rio Grande and rode into Mexico in the last days of the war, hoping to found a new empire of Southernness with a Spanish lilt, over on the Pacific Coast. Anything was preferable to the humiliation of surrender, even when surrender made all kinds of sense, and this is the sort of thought process that afflicts us Redmonds to this day.

The new empire, called Carlotta, never took, didn't work out, and eventually those unsurrendered Missouri boys who lived through all the extra killing this empire scheme had required, straggled back home and became hotheaded democrats and occasional outlaws.

General Jo and Uncle Bill took the loss of the Redmond

land, land that would have eventually been theirs, about the same way those other rebels took the loss of the Confederacy. General Jo and Uncle Bill had dreams of buying back their vast acres, and they applied for an unsecured loan of sorts on payroll day at The Sunnyside Dairy near Lebanon. They made their applications with shotguns in hand and stockings over their faces. They managed a clean getaway, and all was well for about two weeks, until Uncle Bill's wife caught him having at it with a car hop from the Dog'N Suds. In her instant miff, she went overboard, ratted them both out to the law. General Jo and Uncle Bill were in the Missouri pen from just before I was born, and I didn't really know General Jo until he came home when I was seven, and I have still never called him "Dad" to his face. General Jo has never done serious time again, just a few overnights in the drunk tank. Uncle Bill, a recidivist fuckup, stayed free less than two years before catching life for a straight-razor fandango he instigated at The Inca Club with his ex-wife's new husband.

I ofttimes feel that my genes have me cornered.

Because, hand to heart, ever since that round of golf at which I'd triumphed by virtue of a single, perfectly lucky stroke that smacked the cow-pattie stack, I'd smelled that smell. That smell of the not too savory but awfully attractive that seemed always to perfume the times Smoke and me spent together. The stink of self-expressive and unapologetic wrongness, a stink I'd whiffed young, been weaned on in fact, found intoxicating, and had come to miss.

My answer reflected my needs.

8

Skid Marks

Cupid was a silent partner in this criminal conspiracy, or maybe it was that gnat-ball destiny, as Niagra got tagged to break me in, show me the layout of the money garden. Big Annie kept a little Toyota pickup in the barn, and Niagra brought it up to the house, around the side where the hose hooked up. An old water-bed husk lay in the bed of the truck, and she brought the hose out and made the connection.

"This takes a while," Niagra said. "We never go water 'til way after full dark. You don't ever know who might see the water bed in the truck and leap to the right conclusion."

Her champagne blond hair seemed like a lightbulb in the moonlight. "Incandescent" would fit. I just enjoyed it so to watch her move in any manner: tiny head shakes, hand brushing her hair, the stances she took. My loins, a region I'd been neglectful of for a spell, gave those tiny tingles, that loose feeling of want. I hadn't been in a sexual scene that didn't feature my right hand as ingenue since California.

"So, Niagra," I said, trying to dredge forth some sort of swain charm, "uh, what's your major?"

"Boy howdy," she said, and a slow smile showed her white teeth in the moonglow, "you're wantin' at my booty so bad you can't hardly speak."

"I can speak, shit."

"No, look," she said, "it's charming. I know I'm hot." She looked to the water mattress, only slowly filling. "And my major is theater arts, but I'm never goin' to graduate."

"Sure you will."

"No. You don't get it. I'm takin' my share of all this and goin' out to actin' school in Hollywood."

"You might just make it," I said.

"Really?" she said, and for that instant she fairly bloomed with wild hope. "I'm ecstatic with that. That's mighty good to hear, comin' from an artist like you, Doyle." She did a sort of curtsy that made her chest-puppies frisky behind that T-shirt. "Molto grazie."

"Prego," I said.

"Parle italiano?"

"No."

"Good," she said. "Me neither. I can only say one sentence, and it's not one that'll take me far."

"What is it?"

"Il gatto è grande."

I lit a Lucky, then laughed.

"I see the problem with that," I said. "It might function as an icebreaker at somebody's house who has cats. Other'n that, I don't see the future in it."

She leaned over the truck, patted the water mattress. There were two inches of road dust caked on the bumpers, and she tried not to lean on the dirty parts.

"You know," she said, over her shoulder, "if you shaved those crappy goatee whiskers off, you wouldn't look half bad."

"Not half bad, huh."

"Cute," she said. "You're not that young, but without those whiskers I wouldn't see you so much as not that young. More as just cute, period."

"I reckon I'll run in and shave this minute."

That got her to laugh, and laughter is the opening wedge to carnal tomfoolery, so my lower parts actually experienced one or two anticipatory throbs.

"Come on now, Doyle. We've got work to do."

She said it like she meant it, and she did.

Those water beds take a long wait to fill. Damned Spot kept coming around, making herself available for petting, but I'd had a surfeit of dog interaction. I went into the house and fetched a can of Stag from Big Annie's fridge. Smoke and Big Annie were in the front room, laughing hard at some show they'd pulled in off the satellite dish. It might've been *Arsenio Hall*, because Smoke said, "That brother's jokes hit splat on my funny bone. More so than them white boys. I don't know why."

I left them to their beamed-in mirth, went back outside. I stood there, sipping beer, while Niagra sat in the truck with the door open. Over at the porch light a jamboree of june bugs and so forth were tapping out an insect jig against the light shade and the screen door. At one point, for some reason, Niagra told me she'd been named not for the honeymoon spot but for the movie of that title. I didn't know the flick, but we chewed the fat that way for a bit, listening to water gurgle into the mattress.

At some likely moment I inquired as to why she didn't have a fella.

"These fellas hereabouts are just too un-fuckin'-couth," she said. She sidled over, took a sip of my beer. "Plus, I just look around at how folks here wind up, and alls I can say is, Thank God for Greyhound, you know? I see girls I know here and there, and now they got double-wide butts and bad hairdos and off-kilter kids they take government money for. The husbands all seem to not wash too often, but they're tush-hog masters in their own trailer homes, you know, and don't ever take *no guff* off their women. So you see the women at the IGA with jacked-up eyes and split lips 'cause they couldn't wash the skid marks out of hubby's rancid undershorts, more skid marks in there than you see at the Indy 500." She took another sip of my beer, then sighed and fell back against the truck. "It just ain't been heart-rendering for me to say and say and say, 'I'm washin' my hair tonight—I think I'll pass.'"

I said, "That's something I don't ever have, skid marks in my undershorts."

"That's 'cause you don't wear no undershorts."

"How in the hell can you know that?" I asked, and I was sincere.

"Oh," she said, "the way your pecker lays out against your leg, there. Plus, Smoke is the same way, so I recognize the look." She smacked the water mattress then, and the smack made a deep sound. "That's full enough," she said. "Let's do the job."

9

Cast a Goomer

The money garden had been planted in an idyllic spot. Niagra showed the way, steering the lugging Toyota down the rock road a half mile at first, which was the part of the course where the chance of accidentally being spotted was highest. Then, at the slab bridge over a seasonal creek called Gum Creek, she steered down the bank and onto the dry bed. Gum Creek only runs on rainy days and was full of rocks, every different size short of huge. Niagra killed the headlights but knew the way blind. She kept the pace down and bounced us along in low gear.

I'm not sure how much distance we'd traveled before she turned up the low lip of the creek bank and took us in among the deep gloom of the tall trees. When she stopped, she flicked the headlights on, illuminating the money garden.

"There she is," Niagra said.

The patch was planted beneath open spots in the tree

limbs above, so as to receive good sunlight but be a little harder to spot from a chopper. It looked to be eighty or ninety green stalks of reddish-bud dope, spread out down a slope with southern exposure. The plants were mingled among legal flora so as not to stand out. The crop looked to me to be close to harvest, standing five and a half feet tall or thereabouts. That red weed doesn't tower, which is an advantage in concealing it.

Niagra doused the lights and said, "What do you think?"

"It's close to harvest," I said, and I was glad to have that ladystinger in my belt. "Rip artists would likely say it's ready now."

"It's not, though. Ten more days should do it."

"What strain is it?"

"The strain, that's a sad story," Niagra said. "Big Annie paid out quite a li'l bit of cash for a bottle of sinsemilla seeds, only it's not sinsemilla. That's a score to settle later. It's just Razorback Red, that Afghan strain."

"Razorback Red," I said, "I like pretty well."

"It's fine enough," she said. "Good enough everyday dope. But, man, that sinsemilla'd be worth double, at least."

The Ozarks are rampant with dope patches. An article in the *West Table Scroll* had said that the average income for an Ozark family of four was right at twelve thousand dollars per annum, and with economics such as that shouting encouragement, all stripes of old and young in the hills had taken to dropping down those magic seeds that were worth a thousand bucks per plant, at minimum, when ripe. It's crime, but it's also tradition and common sense.

55

Daniel Woodrell

We got out and Niagra ran a hose from the water mattress into the garden. She gave that hose a long suck I coveted to start the water flowing. She then connected our hose to a nozzle that peeked out of the dirt. This was the irrigation system: hoses lightly buried and running among the cash plants. Then she said, "This'll make a crop. All the males were choked off early, before they mingled with the gal weeds and weakened 'em."

About then, my brain charted the geography involved and I knew where we were.

"This is our land," I said. "Our old land."

"Byrum land now," Niagra said. Then she repeated the first rule of wacky backy croppin'. "Always grow on somebody else. We thought, Who is least likely to have his acres tromped all up and down by the snoopy law?"

"Choppers might still fly over."

"We'll just have to roll the dice on that."

The hose gurgled into the garden. We moved it now and then, to other nozzles, as the purpose was only to heal the dried cracks in the ground, not drown the patch.

Niagra was a lovely vision, even in the dark. Not long before the watering was done she said, "If a married fella was to go for me, I couldn't blame him. I don't never dish out guilt. Guilt ain't on my menu." She sighed at the folly of her fellow man, who succumbs to guilt, or I guess that's what it was, then said, "Guilt, what is it, anyhow?"

"Consciousness of doin' wrong," I said. "Assumin' you feel badly about doin' wrong."

"I don't consider what I ever do as ever wrong. I operate in the full range of my spirit. That can't be wrong."

There is nothing like youth for uttering reckless, abso-

56

lutist pronunziamentos. How I longed to share a pure belief in them.

I didn't want to say something too experienced and inappropriate, so I merely smoked and listened. Later, as she rolled up the hose, I said, "It's hard to be good."

"Bein' good ain't ever good enough," she said. "Bein' *bad* doesn't necessarily even get the job done. Good or bad, whatever your dream is, it's gotta catch fire somehow." I could tell she was looking right at me when she spoke. "You should understand that, Doyle. Your books are as good as any I know, but you never had a hit, have you?"

"No, I haven't."

"That's 'cause you need to catch fire somehow."

"Yeah, I know," I said, and man, did I. "I need a hook. A publicity hook. 'Doyle Redmond is the true voice of the ABC Generation,' or whatever. 'A kingfish poet who channels tales of yesteryear's fragrant underbelly.' Something that'll get some key profiles written. Something that'll get the public imagination keen on me. I really need that hook."

In the truck a while after, driving blind on the creek bed, she said, "Could be you've met your hook, Doyle. Hold on to your hat."

The gang decided to bunk me in the spare mobile home alongside the deck. There was a bed in what should've been the kitchen that had a few lumps in it but would do well enough. That was it as to furnishings, as the trailer basically was a storage bin, crammed with boxes and furniture that had no usefulness until somebody got around to doing a mass of repair jobs.

I liked it okay.

My move-in was swift. I had only the blue pillowcase of my traveling clothes and one box of books in the Volvo trunk. I immediately displayed the books on the kitchen counter, as these books I never left behind and made any crap hole I landed in home to me. There were a couple of Elizabeth Bowen novels, a quartet by Edward Lewis Wallant, one volume of Pierce Egan's *Boxiana, The Williamsburg Trilogy* by Daniel Fuchs, Carson McCuller's oeuvre, a stack of Twain, a batch of Erskine Caldwell's thin li'l wonders, some Liam O'Flaherty and John McGahern and Grace Paley and Faulkner, all of Chandler, and a copy of Jim Harrison's *A Good Day to Die.* Also, a jumbo volume of Robinson Jeffers poetry, and various guide-works to flora and fauna. Dictionary and thesaurus, of course, and my boot-camp yearbook from Platoon 3039, which would've been my junior year in high school. Plus, copies of my own output.

In about seven minutes I had relocated and settled in cozy.

The next few days were a joy to be in, a series of simple pleasures and funky interludes.

Big Annie expressed concern about my eternal spirit and went about trying to buff it up to full health. She hung a dream catcher over my bed. The bed one night was strangely painful, and I flipped on the light and found crystals under the pillow and mattress. I left them there, and when I thanked Big Annie for the supernal aids she'd planted near me, she said, "You've got an old soul, Doyle. Many lives."

My ears felt hot, hearing that, but I said a lie. "I don't buy into that bullshit."

Some considerable concern was expressed about the safety of the money garden, and Smoke said, "They're too lazy to rip before the harvest, Springer an' those Dollys. If I'm right, they'll let us harvest and square up the pounds, then we gotta worry."

But as a rule, Smoke and me iced down beer in a cooler and played golf close to daybreak to escape the heat. The contests on the cow-pattie links became serious, as competitions between brothers most always do. We belted the balls around that white pasture, acquiring local knowledge of the course, and soon we both broke one forty. The day after, one thirty looked possible. Smoke was the better athlete, but I'd actually played real golf quite a bit with a fellow writer in California, a perfectly mannered societal reject from Palo Alto with a trust fund and several private memberships, so I won every round.

Smoke thought it was unfair, once I let slip about my level of experience.

"But you designed the course," I said. "Nobody designs their own golf course lookin' to be beat on it, either."

"I might just design it over," he said. Then he snatched onto me and lifted me above his head and twirled me, and I had this ghastly Ginger-Rogers-in-distress sensation. Not too many men can do me that way, but I had the great misfortune to have one who can as a brother. He was reminding me of the law of the jungle, which was that he could snap my neck any time the notion seemed agreeable to him. "Make it a combination game," he said, spinning me, "a li'l bit golf, a li'l bit wrestling."

I started to laugh, dizzy, and Smoke did, too. He set me down and I had to squat to get my bearings.

I said, "If you're within six strokes of me tomorrow, it'll be because I took pity on your clumsy ass."

Smoke cocked his head, then grinned.

"That's why I love you, Doyle. You're too fuckin' dumb to know when to quit." He nodded four or five times. "A fella like that might just get something big done, someday."

Niagra slung the hash every evening, but it was never hash. One evening her hillbillyette surprise was pappardelle con il ragù di fegatini, which is a tongue-twister name for broad, homemade noodles with a fabulous chicken-liver gravy. Another night it was coq au vin, which I love anytime. Then she doubled back on my gustatory expectations and eschewed the continental cuisine in favor of navy beans with ham over cornbread, and collard greens and stewed turnips on the side. Real good redneck chow.

She always watched me eat, and it was never a hardship to eat plenty.

After one evening meal, the redneck one, a dusty Chevy sedan passed by on the dirt lane, and Big Annie said, "I bet you anything that's a carload of Dollys, out scoutin' us."

It was an afternoon I was languishing in when I got hit by the kind of impromptu horror that writers fear. That is, Niagra fell by my trailer with a copy of her screenplay. It was hot and I couldn't lie fast enough to get out of it. I took a seat on the deck, muttered something about loving to read it.

She fetched me beers as I turned pages. She only had sixty-some pages written, but I was only on the second beer when the other thing writers fear came true; that is, a total fuckin' amateur you've had your eyes on sticks you with a piece of work close to her heart, and you, despite your years of study and experience, don't know a thing you can do to improve it, or ever make it salable, but you have to come up with some sweet horseshit that can make her smile and be chummy instead of becoming an instant enemy. She'd titled it *Goomer Doctor,* and it was about a girl named Falls who was hippie spawn and lived in the woods with her mother, Large Lucy. Falls was always being shooshed out of the house when Large Lucy had gentlemen callers, so the little girl would climb to the fork of a big tree I could see in the side yard there and fantasize whilst listening to Large Lucy pleasure her company. The little girl's fantasies featured bizarre, companionable forms of wildlife, until the evening she trailed a glowing coyote into the deep woods and the glowing coyote led her to the cave where a male goomer doctor lived. "Goomer doctor" is an ancient hillbilly term for a witch, basically, though they are of any sex. The goomer doctor takes Falls in hand and starts apprenticing her to the dark arts. Only a goomer doctor of the opposite sex can truly bring a new one into the fold. Eventually they must be joined in sexual intercourse to realize the full mojo. Falls is only eleven, and goomer doctor doesn't mean pervert, so there are some years of schoolin' to come before her doctorate of goomers can be realized.

Cut to: Falls at sixteen. She now chants, "Pully-bone

holy-ghost double-yolk! Pully-bone holy-ghost double-yolk!" and similar incantations. The right formula of words to cast goomers have been learned by her. She knows now how to conjure shape-shifting into swamp rabbits or crows, and toss off good charms and evil charms, but she has yet to consummate her doctorate, so her applications of black magic are still entirely theoretical. Then the goomer doctor takes her to the cemetery to confer the total powers on her, bare butt against an infidel's tombstone, but he's gotten up in age and acquired too many hexes of his own and is impotent.

Falls is distraught, even surly.

Then the goomer doctor says he knows of a young buck goomer doctor of considerable powers over by Bull Shoals Lake, and that's where the pages ran out.

Niagra watched me finish and she just stood there, in a red cotton dress, barefoot, awaiting my critique.

"A good read," I said finally. "The format is wrong, and most movies have quite a bit more dialogue."

"Film is a visual medium," she said. "So I went with lots of visual."

"There's only about fifty lines of dialogue, though."

"Yep," she said. "I favor montage."

I stalled. I lit up. I swished the beer can about.

"The goomer stuff is good," I said.

"I'm way into that," she said. She was still standing over me in that red dress and I didn't want to foul my chances of ever getting such a garment off her. "I've studied goomer doctorin' a good deal. There's a lot to it, you know."

"Well, sure."

"That's my big ace," she said. "When I get to Hollywood, why, I'll cast a goomer down Sunset Boulevard, then I'll do one toward Burbank for TV work." She sort of laughed, a bit self-consciously. "If you'd shave, I'd cast a goomer or more for you, too, Doyle. You could stand havin' a good goomer or two on your side, boostin' you along."

Niagra, so full of scrumptious hope, is looking at me, there, afraid I won't share her vision. She's afraid I'll tell her that the world won't let her have her dreams realized quite so easily, and probably not at all. That her dream is just a thread of fantasy to hang by for a while, but it'll go limp one horrid night somewhere down life's road and start coiling around her pretty neck. But I don't want to tell her. I won't do it. Because those young dream-years are by far the best years, when you have hardy faith and gallops of energy and go for it all, perhaps in a dumb fashion but with gusto, right up 'til the night the dream goes limp and starts that coil.

"Yes, ma'am," I said. "That could be my next future."

10

Boogerdog

"You're cute," Niagra said. That compliment was a reward for shedding my whiskers into the sink. "You look three and a half years younger, too."

"Grazie."

We were on the blind stretch of the dry creek bed. There was a half moon and a slight odor of skunk in the night. Something nosy had gotten sprayed. Imaru was being paged, but not distinctly.

Apropos of nothing, except perhaps my graphic telepathic memos, Niagra asked, "Do you go oral on women?"

"Only when I can," I said. "Otherwise, no."

"Huh. I figured as much."

At the money garden we ran the hose out and did the watering job. Neither of us spoke. She was in those shorts again, the ones that almost covered her butt, and those flame-lick boots and a blue halter.

Eventually I spoke up.

"Niagra, I'm only going to warn you this once. Don't tease me, and don't lead me on."

"I hear that."

After the water was all gurgled out, instead of getting in the Toyota, she slithered up right next to me and grabbed my hand.

"I want to show you something," she said. "Come along."

I trailed her like she was a glowing coyote. She'd swept me into her fairy tale. Her hand never left mine, and she led the way through the thick and spooky woods, over a hill and around a pond. Mosquitoes were biting that night and that was the only part of nature that went against the enchanted spell.

I'd say it was fifteen minutes before Tararum came into view. The drumstick palace was lit up clear across the lower story, and citronella candles flickered all about the patio and pool area. You could see shadows moving around, and hear voices and an occasional splash.

"Isn't it beautiful?" Niagra said.

"I guess."

"I see that," she said, "and my whole soul just screams, I want! I want! I want!"

"I've seen better," I said. "Out around Palo Alto and Pacific Heights and Carmel, in California. Mission Hills in K.C."

Her hand squeezed mine excitedly.

"Oh, Doyle," she said, "better'n Tararum would make me faint, I reckon, with all the want that'd be shootin' through me."

She led on again, not toward Tararum but parallel to it.

Her hand steered me across an area of mowed grass, her blond hair shining. She led to a gazebo or cupola or whatever, about a hundred yards from Tararum, near The Howl. It was over a slight ridge from where I'd noodled that bullhead, so I hadn't seen it before, and there was a path from it going straight toward the big house. The gazebo was shaped like a bell, sort of, with a considerable amount of ornate lacework of lumber near the eaves. The floor was six steps from the ground, and up we went.

The gazebo was painted bright white, and with the moon and all, vision wasn't too bad, not exactly in focus but like a gauzy art film. Niagra let go of me, and went to the rail, and stared toward Tararum.

"This is my secret spot," she said.

She had her hands on the rail and stretched her body, and those shorts rode way high on her ass; then she went taller on the toes of those flame-lick boots and those shorts slipped clear up and in like a thong bikini.

I fell to my knees and went right after it.

I encircled her waist from behind and undid the shorts and gave a yank, yanking them down to her knees. She had on white cotton schoolgirl panties, and I just slid those aside, got my nose to her butt and my tongue in her bush. I pushed her forward some for cleaner licking, and after about six tongue flicks her knees sagged and she moaned, then said, "I'm virgin."

My response was, "Mmph."

"I've got to lay down, Doyle, my legs are gone."

I jerked her down to the floor of the gazebo and she shoved her shorts and panties to her knees, and I dove straight in under the tangle of garments and went hungry, hungry, hungry after her virgin muff.

I felt inspired. She was as so much nectar, divine honey, a potion. She was *that* song. My tongue employed the strokes of a Picasso, li'l light flicks on the clit, the lips, then traced tiny, gentle circles around the pleasure button, then up and down. I had both hands under her butt, roaming and squeezing and raising for deep tonguing. Those flame-lick boots were beating against the wooden floor, sounding like a jungle drum, and somebody was beating a piano at Tararum.

"Oh, sin me up," Niagra said. "Sin me up good'n evil."

Suckin' that split, I felt transported, enlightened, only with a huge boner. Those boots kept drumming to the strumming, and when she busted her kicks she fairly screamed an orgasmic hallelujah.

I crawled back, then sat up, breathing hard.

Niagra laid there, looking gorgeous, raunchy, and magical, her eyes closed, her fingertips tweaking at her nipples through her shirt.

"Goodness," she said. "That was weird. I liked it a lot."

I snatched back my wind, and snap, like that, my own nature required reciprocity. I stood, posed in the moonglow so bright in the white gazebo, and unbuckled. My bird dog stood out, on a hard point toward her brunette bush.

Niagra looked up, then baffled me.

"What're you doin'?" she asked. Immediately, instinctively, she began to scurry. She jumped up and jumped up her garb and buttoned it. "What're you thinkin', Doyle?"

"I don't get your confusion, here."

"I ain't ready for that," she said. "That's the whole hog." She took baby steps backward. "It's important I stay virgin."

"I hope that's the punch line," I said. " 'Cause this best be a joke."

She bit her lip. She lowered her face. She tossed her mane.

"I've got to lose my cherry accordin' to the bylaws," she said. "I'm serious about my goomerin', Doyle. It's got to be in a cemetery at midnight."

"Didn't I warn you about this?"

"Well, yeah, listen, though. I have to say the Lord's Prayer backwards at the tombstone of an infidel, and fire seven silver bullets, then . . ."

I lunged and she scampered, high-booting down the steps and across the mowed grass, toward the deep woods. She glowed away into the dark thicket.

Niagra left me there, in the shadows and the pits, in a molten state of thwarted desire, on the brink of a major testosterone tantrum.

Four Luckies later I arrived at the truck. I was in a blue-balled snit. I told her to shove her silly ass over and let me drive. She didn't argue. She shoved over and I saw her hand was on the latch, ready to flee.

I punished the Toyota, running her mean down the creek bed blind, four or five times as fast as Niagra drove. We were in rich dark made by the tunnel of trees that sagged over the creek bed and leaned against one another in the middle. I kept staring at her as I drove, rocks thumping against the undergut and fenders, the truck bouncing high and wild, but she stayed against the far door, clinging, eyes shifty.

"How could you do me like that?" I asked. She wouldn't meet my eyes. "Look at me, would you?"

Niagra turned her head toward me, her expression a clotted frown, then she looked out the windshield and her mouth dropped. Her hand came up to aim through the glass in alarm, but before her message reached me there was a weighty thump and something skidded wet and heavy across the hood and over the windshield.

"What on earth was that?" I asked.

"Boogerdog!" she screamed.

"Deer, maybe."

"Boogerdog!" she said. "Boogerdogs are always around, provokin' fiendish events."

"Will you shut the fuck up with your goomers and your boogerdogs and shit! Please!"

She spoke more quietly next time.

"Boogerdog. I saw its paw scrape across the windshield."

11

Boiled Onion Eyes

I have a sense I'm living in more than one world at a time and they're all out to get me. Wicked worlds. Vindictive. Parallel and relentless worlds bullying me now for whatever bad acts I pulled when I was other people in other epochs.

That's just the sense I have. It's a sense of being haunted full-time that makes for a certain amount of midnight anguish and round-the-clock creeps.

The scene in the barn after the boogerdog encounter was one where I felt stuck in a cusp, hung between various worlds, I guess, and I saw everything happen as from an aerie, a cold distance, for I was there, but then again, I wasn't.

I left the headlights on when I slammed the truck inside the barn. The light beams played off the grayed wood and gave a glow to the interior. I got out, went to the Toyota hood to check for damage, or a raccoon tail in the grill, maybe, or a tuft of deer hide.

Some words passed my lips, something like, "There's no special damage."

Then Niagra screamed. She was still sitting in the cab but looking out the rear window to the truck bed, and her scream got mixed with oaths and moans coming from behind her.

I hustled over, gave a look, and felt sick.

In the truck bed there was a man in black. One leg was busted above the ankle and white bone protruded, and the below-the-ankle part of the leg seemed to be stepping in the wrong direction. Plenty of blood. And the man's face was rising like bread dough, swelling big from the cheeks to the hairline, only purple in hue. The man didn't seem too large, nor too young, but all wrecked, and his eyes were of that blue type, with extra white, filmy around the blue. Boiled onion eyes.

Niagra shouted, "That's a Dolly! That's a fuckin' Dolly!"

The man in black had a problem in the shoulder area; his right arm just flopped there, limp. There was a pale tattoo of a huge spider between the thumb and forefinger on the hand that went with that arm.

I stalked out of the barn, into the night. Then I stood there, and ten thousand lightning bugs were flickering away across the countryside. The dog loped by, into the barn, and Niagra shuffled out. She draped her arms around me from behind, rested her head on my shoulder. We stood like that, together, trembling, trying to reach out for our composure.

"It's down to the nut cuttin', now," I said.

"I know," she said. "You ain't a false alarm, are you?"

"I wonder."

Back in the barn, Damned Spot, her tail swishing, was jumping back and forth over the man in black, who had dragged his wrecked self out of the truck to the dirt and had begun crawling. That broken bone wiggled as he crawled, and he bellowed.

"Damn," I said.

The man kept crawling, and a scarifying question hit me. Are all Dollys as dead game as this one?

Niagra stepped up, put her boot to the man in black and rolled him over onto his back. The roll earned a scream.

"I don't know his name," the girl said, "but he's one of the ringleader Dollys."

The man spit at her and she jerked backward, out of spittin' range.

Those boiled onion eyes stared up, alive with fierce agony. His left hand pawed at his beltline.

"I can't stand this," Niagra said. "We need to extend mercy to this man."

"Mercy?"

"Uh-huh. A hole in the head that ends his misery."

"I don't know if I can be like this."

"Let me enhance upon my point," Niagra said. "He's a Dolly out here scoutin' us for a rip-off, so we can't let him go."

"But, just killin' him, I don't know."

The ladystinger is in my pocket. Niagra takes it.

"You figure we could nurse him back to health like a sick bunny or somethin'? Then release him back to the woods?"

"Hold your mud," I said. Then, what could I do except

72

look down at the Dolly, and the Dolly's boiled onion eyes were terrible, full of hurt but committed to ruin. "Shit, he's got a pistol."

The Dolly made a feeble try to raise a revolver, a thirty-eight, with his left hand, but his thumb appeared broken or sprung. He was making slow progress. His eyes fixed on me, his selected target, and this intense attention caused me to freeze. The writer's disease, that of preferring acute observation to action, had seized me up. I'd gone still in a trance of observations, noting the way the Dolly's mouth tugged to the right, a tuft of whiskers below the nose the razor had missed and were gray, while the head hair was black, only a few lines of gray, and the black T-shirt the man had on featured a St. Louis Cardinals emblem, red, in the heart zone, and he'd gotten purchase on that revolver, finally, and raised it above his belt buckle, a buckle that sported a horse head in profile inside a horseshoe, and I, the writer, just stood there, frozen, trying to get a prose poem, a conte, out of this event that might well climax with my being shot.

Niagra crouched forward with the ladystinger and let off a round. She scored the downed Dolly in the belly, then moaned and dropped the ladystinger and it did a short cartwheel before resting in the dust.

The dog fled about here.

The gunshot had gotten the Dolly to drop his pistol, but he wasn't dead.

I picked the ladystinger from the dust, and the girl just bellowed about mercy, and the Dolly kept trying to crawl across the straw and dirt of the barn floor.

I believe I said, "Tonight ain't exactly my first rodeo— but I've never done anything like this before. Me'n Smoke pulled a couple of things where we showed our guns, but never used them. Once, when I was at KU, gettin' my bachelor's in English, a rock'n roll fella, a drummer, had shorted me on a jar of speed and I shoved a pistol in his ear, but that boy saw the light."

"Cut!" Niagra screamed. "Cut!"

The crawling man in black hadn't gotten very far, his miserable passage charted by a blood trail in the dirt.

"Aw, Imaru," I said. Then I sighted in on the Dolly and emptied the ladystinger into his back, li'l plumes of blood splashing up in the kind of li'l splashes pennies make when tossed into a wishing well. "There's your mercy, girl."

12

Peace in the Valley

It could well be that you've shouldered a drunk boyfriend up the front steps a time or two on pay night, or swooped your lady love from the kitchen to the boudoir, but the dead weigh different. There are no helpful staggers or neck hugs for balance. Even the smallish dead, I learned, have this obstinate, lumpish heft to them.

Carrying the corpse into the woods fell to me, as either an earned right or a punishment or a spiritual duty, I'm not certain, but the decision was silently made and mutual. I did the fireman carry, which is easier, but I felt Dolly blood running down my back and could hear creepy interior gurgles and poot noises from the corpse so near to my ear.

Smoke led the way, carrying a small flashlight and a hogleg magnum on the chance there might be more Dollys lurking about. Big Annie, showing a shading of her personality not exactly in the hippie groove, swung a twelve-gauge pump and seemed fairly expert in its usage. Niagra brought the shovel, and she had a quiet case of the mumbles. She was uttering whispered nonsense, likely, probably grandiose goomers, but her step was light.

We were not on a trail, as trails attracted walkers, but were cutting through tangled forest, and this made me work hard, tugging the Dolly through briar traps and low limbs and across the uneven earth. I enjoyed the physical expense, the effort, as it calmed me as Doyle, but I was enveloped by an embrace of spiritual certainty that Imaru was not unfamiliar with such occasions.

The shots had still been singing in my ears when Smoke and Big Annie came rushing into the barn. They took in the scene quickly, came to the correct conclusions without speaking, and Smoke hugged my neck while Big Annie did likewise on her daughter.

Niagra ran down the chain of events to the rest of the gang, in amazingly cool and precise sentences, with concrete details, while I wavered between worlds, experiencing a druggy kind of confusion as to which century I currently haunted. I had just absorbed raw and terrible insight about Imaru, who I realized was an eternal misfit and hothead set loose in time, and his/her problems with every world he/she passed through. This fresh self-awareness ironed out any hopeful doubts about the future.

I hoped my next-life penance could be as a dog, a pampered, coveted breed, who could chase a pastry wrapper from Zabar's out an Upper West Side window or something, and set things straight with the spirit world by splattering on an exclusive sidewalk.

"The spider, there," Smoke said. He hunkered down and raised the right hand of the dead man. "That spider is famous. It belongs to a mean Dolly they all call Bunk. I think this is Bunk, anyhow."

"It's him," Big Annie said. "That face sort of looks like him."

"Sort of looks like him if he'd been hit by a truck, at least."

At this point Smoke laughed, and it was not a comforting laugh in tone or volume. Smoke's laughter seemed to belittle the deceased somewhat, and then he explained the famous spider inked on the dead man's hand.

Bunk Dolly was a remainder of one of the several Dolly tribal units that had squatted on National Forest land in the thirties, over by the Twin Forks River, just off BB Highway, and had been allowed to stay permanently when the process of evicting them all turned out to be far more perilous than was worthwhile. These BB Dollys are revered by some and resented by others, as their penchant for arson and ambush had resulted in such a sweet real estate deal, to their sole benefit. They've been there ever since, raiding their neighbors' barns and hog pens from prime forest acres they'd never put a penny down on in payment.

Bunk must've been about forty-three, and he'd followed the Dolly career track in an exemplary fashion. He climbed the Dolly rungs happily, it appeared. Reformatory bits, county jail time, then the big top in Jeff City, where there are probably enough Dollys to make a chorale group. Like many a dumbass career criminal, ol' Bunk had allowed himself to be boogered up with readily identifiable tattoos, which of course heightened the odds of quick return to the chorale group after each release.

Seven or eight months back he'd been in a halfway house in Kansas City with only six weeks to go when he

decided to escape, and inevitably he escaped to BB Highway and started robbing country markets. The last job he
pulled was in West Table, where he took off Caulkins
Grocery over by the high school. He'd picked up some fine
points of criminal mastery, and wore a Halloween mask, a
scarf around his neck, and sunglasses over his eyes behind
the mask, but when he raised his chopped 410 single-shot
toward the store clerk it must've hit him he'd forgotten his
gloves. He let go with a blast of birdshot, but the clerk, a
gal named Chichester I'd gone to school with, wasn't
killed, merely ruined forever.

The spider on his hand had the crime solved in about
ninety seconds, and Bunk had remained in hiding
amongst his tribe ever since.

I understood, now, why Smoke laughed.

"That makes me feel more okay about killing him," I
said. "Me'n Paula Chichester, hell, we went from kinder-
garten on up together."

"You should feel fine about it," Big Annie said. "Karma
is as karma does."

"I didn't even know Paula'd been shot," I said. "Jesus.
In science class she was the girl who kissed the Jell-O, you
know, so we could study how mold'd grow even from a
pretty girl's kiss. It did, too. Younger, I recall, Paula always
did really dig that kickball game, could boot the ball to the
fence. This son of a bitch, here, had it comin'. I mean, shit,
that's clear-cut, *ain't* it?"

The nature of our region made digging the hole a long
stretch of miserable spade work. The rocks, the thinness of
the soil, the roots running everywhere the shovel stabbed.
The grave never did reach regulation proportions. When

we tired out it was still fairly shallow and maybe a foot shorter than it needed to be.

We were all sweated up and gamey in the heat, stinking of mortal dread and adrenaline and plain effort.

The Dolly got crammed into the grave, tight fit that it was, his head bent over to where the other head would've been if he'd had a Siamese twin.

Dirt and rocks were flung over him, then we gathered bigger rocks to top off the burial, seal the grave. The last thing we needed was for coyotes to get at him for a feast and leave his leftovers near roads or trails, to prompt speculation among humans on whose leg is this? or this skull? or that spider looks familiar.

Oddly, to my mind anyhow, Smoke started singing a spiritual over Bunk Dolly. His selection was "Peace in the Valley," a real meaningful church tune, though none of us could be considered churched-up folks.

The whole gang of us joined in on the opening of the hymn in decent harmony, but after that first line or two confusion set in as to the lyrics, and the singing became ragged and pitiful, maybe blasphemous.

Niagra sighed. "Please, stop! This singin' is a flop—we don't know the words, and he don't deserve 'em if we did."

Smoke dropped the song in midstanza.

"You're right, hon," he said. "Piss on him."

13

Clawfoot Wash

I stood on the cedar deck for quite a spell, eye-fuckin' the night sky, trying to stare down the stars. Blood had crusted on my neck, back, in my hair, down the legs of my jeans, to where I was as spattered as a thumbless beef packer. I kept on with my close study of the higher reaches, fantasizing that a comet was due to streak by trailing a message meant only for me, spelled out clearly and printed huge. Some epigram from way out there that'd clue me in on how to feel after killing a man.

My feelings so far were pretty much tilted toward the okay, and the remainder shaded toward the So what? That's the feeling that's most wilting, sad, like long, slow cello music played in the lowest register. Hollow. Death don't mean diddly to the wide world, or, as Mister Stephen Crane more or less said it, at the most it creates no sense of obligation in the universe.

But I felt I had come to know a few telling anecdotes

and salacious footnotes concerning the universe, and one certain fact about the eternal: it just keeps coming.

The screen door slapped and I turned toward it. The whole gang stood there, bunched together in the square of light coming from the kitchen. Smoke stepped toward me, then put both big hands on my shoulders and pressed me into a chair. He raised my leg and pulled my left boot off, then the right.

"Strip," he said.

"Say again, bro?"

"Your duds, Doyle. They're evidence. They need to be burned."

For a moment I sat there unmoving, thinking that though we were a gang, this solo stripping act on my part would indicate a new level of gang intimacy. Once I had been goaded by single-malt scotch and sinsemilla into stripping for my wife and two of her girlfriends, believing I was laying the table for one of the most memorable sex feasts of my life, the kind you read about rock stars having, but when I was bared down to the skin I was born in, the ladies pelted me with popcorn and turned on a video of *Mildred Pierce*. As I retreated, stoned and confused, my wife said, "I told you he would."

This, however, was not figuring to be a repeat of that sort of brutal ruse, so I stood, then pulled my shirt over my head. My acquiescence set the gang in motion. Big Annie said she'd run the water and went inside, while Niagra grabbed my boots and said she'd shine the blood spots out. I emptied my jeans pockets, pulled my belt loose, and that was it.

Smoke carried the bloody clothes to the barbecue grill

81

and made a loose mound of them. He squirted starter
fluid on them in heavy splashes.

I fired a Lucky with a wooden match, then dropped the
flame to my duds. The fire took hold slowly at first, then
there occurred a sudden whoosh and I watched naked as
my clothes became a ball of fire. The heat column rose and
made the wind chimes tinkle.

The flame excited the peacocks up in their roosts, and
they gave out cries that set my skin scurrying.

Smoke said, "I'm proud to be your brother, Doyle. I
truly am. Now go take your bath."

I skittered naked into the house. Niagra had gone to
work on my boots and didn't look up. I went into the
bathroom, and the huge clawfoot tub was filled. A candle
burned by the sink.

The water temp was as high as I could stand, and the tub
had the size that allowed a man to stretch out. These old
clawfoot tubs are the only kind I've encountered that
make bathing an actual pleasure. I'd spent the hottest
summer in Kansas history, thirty some straight days that
crested the century mark on thermometers, in an upstairs
apartment with a clawfoot tub. Candles melted, peanut
butter became a beverage. Whole families were sleeping in
the air-conditioned public library, and old folks were
dying as if heatstroke was a Kansas fad. That tub had kept
me alive and sane, as I filled it with cold water and lived in
it from mid-afternoon to near midnight. I drank Falstaff
from an ice chest and read the likes of Turgenev and Jackie
Susann, D. H. Lawrence and Mickey Spillane, until the
heat broke. That clawfoot had been my salvation.

Big Annie came into the bathroom. I had begun to see

her as a sister-in-law, pretty much, except her hippie sunbeam of personality and earthy physique had a tingle of attraction for me. She had her shirt off and a loofah in her hand. Her nipples had the circumference of coffee cups.

She bent over the tub and dunked the loofah, and started lathering me up. She covered me in soapsuds.

"I used to be a nurse's aide," she said, "so relax."

"Is that right?"

"No. But I figured it'd put you at ease if I said so."

She washed me like I was a fresh-born babe, or an ancient man who'd lived too long. I was neither, or both, but I gave myself up to her cleansing ministrations, and the sensation was entirely soothing, warm, and intimate.

When she scrubbed my jewels, I saw Smoke in the doorway, grinning like a coon in the roastin' ear patch. She stroked that loofah across all my secret regions. After that, she shoved my head underwater, raised me back, and began to wash my hair. She pruned for ticks as she rubbed.

"You have nice hair," she said.

On the second round of shampoo Niagra came in. She was biting a thumbnail, to keep from giggling, I think. Then she took her thumb out, giggled, and said, "I've done your boots."

Big Annie's Big Annies bobbled against my wet skin quite a few times, but I felt no stir.

"There's a towel," she said when I was clean. "Get out when you want."

"I'll kill another man tomorrow, Big Annie, if it means you'll do this again."

She toweled her wet bosom, then laughed full throat.

"Stop it," she said.

I did not linger long in the soapy water. I wanted my bed. A warm, heavy fatigue had come over me. I wore the towel to my trailer.

At the bed, I laid out in a manner that brought me into contact with every crystal. I needed them all. I stared up at the dream catcher, watched it flutter in the night breeze.

Sleep almost had me when Niagra slid in beside me. No speech seemed required. We wrapped together, hugged tight, and her breath broke against my neck and her heart beat beneath my hands.

I believe we spent the whole long night held strongly in one another's arms, without so much as a mumbled promise or a sneaky kiss to spoil the purity of our electric, loving cuddle.

14

The Pennies Tell All

When the sun woke me, Niagra was sitting on the edge of the bed, studying me. She looked more beautiful than I deserved. "Doyle," she said. "I've got to know just one thing—what's the deal with your wife?"

After the third straight slow song my wife had danced in the arms of the visiting poet, I figured it was time to find my suitcase in the garage and wipe away the cobwebs. They were dancing to Smokey Robinson in a groin-grinding, rhythmic ballet d'amour that publicly rubbed my nose in their affair. Clearly it had been more than merely their minds meeting in his guest cottage on campus the last week or so. He was the visiting Big Name for the summer poetry workshop, and she the host, so they were supposed to have been evaluating manuscripts. But as I watched that nice, hard can of hers shake and jook, I knew those cottage

walls had heard some recent howling and seen red fingernails raking along sweaty flesh.

The party had dwindled down to half a dozen faculty
sipping wine, and a few student poets overdrinking to
display their intensely troubled, lyric soulfulness. A couple
of the faculty sorts glanced at me, nervously I thought, no
doubt expecting me to hop up and demonstrate my white-
trash temperament by essaying something savage with the
fondue pot.

My seat was across the room from where the lovebirds
danced, my arm resting on a TV set that had the screen
turned to the wall in case an actual wild party occurred.
This bash took place in the home of one of Lizbeth's
colleagues at Hichens College, and there were still a few
Corona beers in the fridge.

I can't say why I wasn't more upset.

I have fallen off a cabbage truck, maybe, but not
yesterday. I knew my wife really needed to fuck this
legendary dude, so I tried to chalk it up to the vicissitudes
of the literary life, or, more to the point, of my life.
Lizbeth danced like liquid, undulating and unfettered by
care, or bra or undies probably. She'd been in a frenzy to
be a poet who was both revered and lusted after ever since
I met her. A hybrid of Edna St. Vincent Millay, Carolyn
Forché, and Gypsy Rose Lee. She was definitely talented,
but not enough so to indulge in self-destructive monoga-
my, and I no longer even wanted her to. This man,
Chamberlin Post, could make her name known, boost her
poetry, grease the skids under a fat grant or two, and
muscle the quarterlies until they reviewed her work. Those
were basically Lizbeth's short-term goals.

I couldn't help her with any of those things, or even the

rent, lately. So, what my wife was doing over in the dark corner was mean and vain and absolutely the right move for her, letting the visiting Big Name familiarly rub her ass with his bony red hands.

Chamberlin Post was one of those commandingly tall, silver-haired, Cape Cod sailor-aristocrats with a lean, blade face of sharp features and gin blossoms budding on his cheeks. He'd taken nearly all the awards except the Nobel, I guess. He'd had most of the gaudy adventures money can make happen: surfing the dangerous coast of Peru, the standard mystical journey up the Amazon, scuba diving the Red Sea, and on and on. There always seemed to be a photographer nearby when he came up out of the drink, or the thick bush, or down from the mountains, and some of the pictures were famous. His poetry concerned forbidden love in Third World circumstances, the often unapprecia-ted social burdens the born-too-rich had to shoulder, and foreign peasants he had come to know on a deeply spiritual level. Most of his work was very good, which distressed me. A lot of personal publicity attached to him because of the famous adventurer pictures and his status as a Brahmin poet.

Of course I thought about kicking his ass. My mammy dropped me in the Ozarks and I'm an Ozarker wherever life takes me. I thought about kicking his ass, but, one, he was a big ol' hoss, and, two, he came from the sort of bluebloods who consider kidnapping a real possibility, so they'd probably made the butler shuttle him to kung fu classes from the age of six or so. One and two put together added up to a weapon. I'd need a weapon, maybe a Corona bottle with a lime wedge in the bottom, to take him down hard. And a weapon certainly meant that a warrant on a felony assault beef would be chasing me after I swept the cobwebs from that suitcase in the garage and launched myself into the California night.

Truly, though, my main feeling was a horrible sense that I owed this man, should thank him, for hammering a simple point home to me: I plain ol' did not belong in or around the academic world, nor with a woman who did. Ever since Lizbeth bought herself a yellow Volvo I knew our dream of surviving solely as writers was entirely defunct, as Volvo ownership functions in practically the same way as a union card for junior faculty at liberal arts colleges. It was a sign of commitment to tenure tracks and seminars and Napa Valley wine. All she'd need now was an Irish setter named Genet or Woolf. Lizbeth would never even let me drive the Volvo, either, as I have this destructive, love-hate relationship with automobiles.

Maybe Chamberlin Post was the final shred of proof that it was truly time to roll my white-trash self back to the low-rent world that spawned me and find some raw subject matter.

I left my beer bottle on the TV set and made my way to the exit. Somebody from among the nervous faculty gave me a pat on the back as I went out the door and onto the lawn. The music followed me—more happy Motown from our childhood. The grass was dry and a little long, and huge eucalyptus and fir trees loomed at the edge of the yard, making this seem like a mystical forest clearing on a Celestial Seasonings box.

The night weather was balmy, no Northern California fog in sight. A fir tree, bigger than the rest, lured me to lay beneath it, so I did.

I knew she'd seen me leave.

I knew she'd want to say some words over us if I laid out on the ground and closed my eyes and waited.

I don't know why I didn't feel worse about everything.

We'd met at a party, too, only it was a very large and nasty party, lots of fun. That had been in Iowa City (Fuck City in that era), Iowa, grad-school days. The party took place in an old sagging Victorian, a former bordello of many rooms, on Clinton Street next to the railroad tracks. One of the rooms had been mine. Over two hundred people were partying in the house, and I'd been tracking Lizbeth for quite a while before I edged through the crowd and got next to her. She was in the poetry work-shop, I knew that, and she made the saliva sizzle on my tongue. I got next to her finally up against a wall in the formal dining room, a huge open space crammed with dancers who made the windows rattle. Lizbeth held a pint of the Glenlivet and stared at one of the faculty honchos who was trying to wrangle a dance with a girl poet who didn't like boys, and he was quite comical, charging his boyish charm relentlessly into the stone wall of her sexual preference.

Lizbeth eventually took her eyes from him, looked at me briefly, a mere glance, then said, "You think I have to fuck him to get a fellowship?"

Those first words really broke the ice. The faculty poet was an imperious li'l tub in his late forties who jiggled when he walked and had a huge messy beard that was supposed to indicate he was too far gone into meaningful thoughts to bother with bourgeois grooming. He special-ized in tiny odes about playing Wiffle ball with his daddy as the Pittsburgh sky grew gloomy, epiphanies he'd had while dieting, and baseball as a metaphor for something I forget. He was unaccountably popular and heavily clapped over in the quarterlies.

"I think if you fuck him you *might* get a fellowship, but you'll damn sure get some sexual memories that'll make you jerk awake in bed, sweating, for the rest of your life."

"Hmm, there might be a good poem in that," she said. She had a bold swig from the bottle of scotch, then gave her eyes over to me. "I've been seeing you everywhere," she said. "The Shamrock, George's, The Foxhead."

"I've seen you, too."

"Yeah, I noticed that. You're Doyle Redmond, the shitkicker from the sticks, and you've got a shitkicker story in *Prairie Schooner.*"

"You've seen it?"

"Yeah," she said. Her light brown hair was long, sensually unbrushed, and her frame would have to be called willowy, I guess. "They say you're the workshop writer most likely to become a prison novelist."

"People here just think I'm dangerous because I didn't go to Antioch or Stanford, or like that."

"You deal dope, don't you?"

"Well," I said, "I'm a writer, and I've been paying my own way a long time now. I live here, in this house."

"Let's go to your room. I want to see how a shitkicker like you lives."

There were strangers screwing in my bed so she didn't get to see how I lived. They were really layin' down some hair, and I only had one sheet, but never mind. I led her onto a side porch that faced the railroad tracks and we sat on a three-legged couch that smelled of mildew. The air was chilly and no one else was out there, and it was one of those times when no preamble of chat seemed required, the lust was running that high, and in under a minute I was finger-bangin' her while she sucked on my ear. Snaps, buttons, buckles, and flaps flew wide, our chemistry being so instant. The music pounded, the walls shook from dancers' feet, and our breath left trails in the air. Two or three times the door opened and there were steps on the porch and laughter or snickers were emitted within a foot of us, but we ignored them, they didn't exist, and we strove after one another on that side porch until the party went quiet near dawn.

Lizbeth Seden, of Pepper Pike, Ohio, and Carleton College, moved her gear into my room just before supper, and we were a mighty strange couple for the next six-plus years, until the night I laid under a California sky, waiting for the last rites to be uttered.

When she sat beside me under that fir tree, she shook my boot toe.

"You're not psyching yourself up to go and be a brute, are you, Doyle?"

"I'm not a brute," I said, not yet opening my eyes.

"You sure can be."

"Why does everybody say that?"

"Because of certain incidents everybody knows about."

I sat up, crossed my legs beneath me.

"When I'm dead they'll say I was 'passionate and ruggedly self-reliant,'" I claimed.

"Oh, Doyle." Lizbeth's lips had that puffy, tender look lips get from deep kissing someone new. "They're not going to talk about you when you're dead."

That sealed the end. That comment. This was the sorest spot she could gouge at, my life's work to this point being four published novels nobody much had read, let alone bought or reviewed prominently. This sore spot of mine had yet to quit oozing since the last book had been met with a great, vicious silence, and for her to stick me there meant it was over for sure.

"Well," I said, "I'd rather disappear into history without even a footprint behind me than fuck Chamberlin Post."

"You never do get it, do you?"

"I think this time I do. You're fuckin' that old sot for your art, right? It's a sign of commitment to your craft and career rather than a betrayal of me."

"That," she said, "is the adult light I would hope you'd see things in."

I felt myself evolving into a poem. A poem being composed as we sat there, the party music in the background, the lover at the party, the huge tree above us, the dry grass, and the marriage that had come to a head. She was entombing me in blank verse while her eyes never left my face, and I hoped to God and the devil I wouldn't ever let myself read it.

"I'll tell you a story," she said. "I think you'll understand it." She put her hands on my leg and bowed her head, her skirt spread wide on the grass. "There comes a boring night, more boring than other boring nights, and with nothing else to do you open your handbag. You find old receipts for things you'd forgotten you owned, come across a stiff stick of gum, a brand they only sell in Mexico, and finally you open your coin purse. You open your coin purse and dump the pennies in your lap, like when you were a girl looking for special pennies that were worth a nickel each to daddy because of their old dates. The older the dates the better, so long as they were older than his little angel. Only on this night you're not a girl anymore, and the game is cruel, like a punch in the tummy, because all the pennies are dated younger than you are now. Not one is from a time before your birth. The girl and the pennies have switched ages, and it comes over you, if you're me and thirty-two on your next birthday, that those young pennies should tell you something. And they do. They tell me it's time to get truly serious about the serious things in life, when a girl finds out she's older than all her fucking pennies."

Big Name stood at the door looking out at us, coughed, then turned away.

"I hear that," I said. "Fuck it."

I kissed her once on her lips so puffy from ambitious kisses, and off she went, gone inside, leaving me there on the lawn, a fresh poem in her wake.

The suitcase in the garage proved impossible to find, but I found a blue pillowcase, and the keys to Lizbeth's prize Volvo.

"That story, it's sad, but it makes me so happy," Niagra said. "That girl has a dream she wants to catch fire, and I can dig that, and root for her. But I'm happy she misdeeded you in her own way, since it shoved you back here for me. I believe we got the makings of a dream that'll burn mighty hot, Doyle, you'n me."

15

Mingled Grease Bucket

Panda's house functioned as a museum of who we once were as a family. Or maybe more of a tomb. I wondered if the seeds of all to come wasn't maintained there in relic form. The house was two-story, nice enough in its day, though its day had passed circa WWII. The wallpaper and drapes are still redolent of a VJ-Day home-decorating sale or something similar. Inherited pieces of furniture are on display and in use throughout, old marble-top dressers, walnut tables, and rocking chairs that have felt the fingers and butts of my people on back to the fin de siècle or even earlier, and have come to know the very same parts of me. There's a closet under the stairs containing firearms, long and short, that have never been let out of the family, though some haven't been fired in my lifetime. The walls in the front and dining rooms are coated with family photographs, the ancestral eyes from a variety of eras always watching, beckoning it seems to me, as if those

94

long-gone hillbilly forebears had a few deep, ugly secrets or harsh, ruinous criticisms they'd love to pass on if I'd stand close enough for whispers.

Imaru felt funny stirrings inside these walls.

The gang had wanted to go shopping, or the distaff wing of the gang anyhow, so I'd dropped the ladies at the square and me and Smoke went to visit Panda.

Panda was out somewhere in the noon heat, on foot and cane, putting his old body in peril. The heat had gotten up to where the cows had all dove into ponds. A man Panda's age should've been hunkered on the shade porch drinking iced tea, but he wasn't.

Smoke, his dreadlocks freshly braided, one of Panda's beers in his hand, studied the wall of our dead. He'd spent more years in this house than I had, and was tied to it by more actual memories than me, though I believe I felt the pull of the blood-kin legends harder.

"Shoo-wee," he said. "There's some nasty motherfuckers in our family tree—know it?"

"I know it."

In the photos there are quite a few fellas in overalls and women in calico. The men wear hats and the women have their hair in severe buns. Redmonds have come always from dirt, worked hard on dirt as a bloodline since probably the days of knights and trolls and wizards and all, long before the U.S.A. even opened for business, so they are all sturdy in appearance. Pinched expressions abound, or happier ones that have a strong hint of predatory gloat to them, often with a nine-point buck at their feet. The ensemble photos were posed so that kids are on one side and the elders on the other, to form a generational fenceline around those in their unbridled prime. There once had been so many Redmonds that quite a few of the faces stumped us as to names. Local Redmonds had since gotten narrowed down by exposure to the outside world. Mostly they'd started migrating on the hillbilly highway to the auto works of Detroit, the oil fields of Texas, or the shipyards of Long Beach back in the thirties, when word reached the hills a man could earn five bucks or more a day in those far-off places.

Our line hereabouts had thinned and thinned, down now to just Panda, and, I guess, us.

"I remember him," Smoke said, jabbing a finger at a rough cob with an eye patch. "One-eyed Garland. The roustabout."

"He used to give us quarters for peggin' rocks at his empty beer bottles."

"That's right," Smoke said, "A quarter if we hit 'em. It was his wife, wasn't it? Over in Oklahoma?"

"Yeah," I said. "Twelve gauge. I think he had it comin'."

"Maybe. He was good to us."

We gave ourselves over to the photos, photos that trailed back to the last century. Before a single beer had been drunk we'd identified seven faces related to us on that wall that we knew for a fact had shot or cut men to death (not counting me), and four that had been on the wrong end of the carnage. Panda's older brother Jeb, for whom Smoke is actually named, had been gutshot near the Jacks Fork in about 1936, never solved. General Jo's favorite first cousin, Doyle, my namesake, had been found in a ditch on the other side of Egypt Grove in 1947. He'd survived the war in the Pacific with the Marines only to get murdered by a sixteen-year-old girl whose heart he'd fiddled with.

I finally turned away from the wall of dead, went to the porch.

It's not always wonderful to ponder the gene pool you squirted from. In a way it's wonderful, I mean, but in six or seven other ways it can make one nervous concerning tragic consistency, ancestral expectations, and that horrible bloodstream urge to go on and do the questionable deeds that might make those dead faces nod in grim approval.

The porch was sideways to the kitchen, the very kitchen in which Smoke had wanted that bacon. General Jo bunked with the state in Jeff City, and we'd lived here with Panda until a few months after his release. Grandma had passed in 1944 and Panda seemed to enjoy us living there. In my mind I could see that hot grease spilling, burning down Smoke's young body, though it might've been legend rather than memory.

"I'm gettin' about to be hungry," Smoke said. He, too, seemed subdued by this house, these walls, the clabbered history. "How 'bout you?"

"Let's wait for Panda."

"Okay. Whatever." Smoke brushed his hand at his dreadlocks. "I reckon I'll take a dump in peace, then."

I dropped to the porch steps and had a cigarette. The brand, Lucky Strikes, took me back to the Marines, as that's where I met the brand and took up the vice. The wall of dead had me thinking, remembering, seeing connections.

I was in boot camp the week I turned seventeen. The folks had moved to K.C., with all its boulevards and fancy strangers and different rules of conduct, and I couldn't stand it; the Corps and possible war exerted more appeal. One evening when I was not yet eighteen and a Lance Corporal Jarhead on Guam, I fell in love with a sweet drink called the Sloe Gin Fizz at The Star Bar on Agana Drive. I overdrank like a puppy will overeat. On the walk outside of the bar, it's midnight or so, and I'm nine thousand miles from the West Table square, and there's an ocean out across the way and palm trees chanting in the breeze. A splendid setting for adventure. Near as I can figure it, from memory and Captain's Mast testimony, this sailor, a total stranger, said a slander about my Jade East aftershave smelling like young pussy, and this ignited some sloe gin fantasy in me about interservice scuffling, fun-loving mayhem, and I apparently took all those thoughts for real and clubbed that Squid down with my fists, then kicked him 'til his ribs caved. It seems I felt I had done something notable and terrific, because I stood over him laughing until the Shore Patrol scooped me up. The man I had tore down in my fantasy turned out to be a Seabee, and something of a war hero. I did my brig time in a strange mood, no longer a lance corporal, sad I'd whipped a hero but sort of proud for jackin' a Seabee, who I considered to be, man for man, the best brawlers in the service of our nation.

This was the sort of incident that repeated itself a few times in life, and got known, and blackballed me from teaching jobs. It was the type of raw act, though, I felt might get that wall of dead to nod in approval.

I didn't want to see it if they did.

Imaru would know.

* * *

When Panda showed, he was grinning a big youthful grin, looking like a severely battered but joyful seven-year-old troll. He came clambering up from the cemetery, using his BB rifle as a cane, carrying two red squirrels by their bushy tails.

Looking at him I thought it must be true that the mighty old can turn suddenly childlike again, as when an odometer on a car turns over and it's back to the first mile once more. Except now it's a decrepit vehicle.

At the porch he lifted the squirrels high and said, "Lunch, boys. You clean, I'll cook."

Panda patted me on the shoulder, a buddy gesture, but wrapped his arms around Smoke and they hugged hard. There's a bond of a special nature between them that's not there between us. Smoke has always been the big delight of Panda's granddaddyhood. He's clearly the brag dog from our litter. There's not even any shit slung about Smoke's hair.

Since I was a toddler it seems I've displayed devious sensitivites that Panda could never take a shine to. I'm a grandson, a direct link, and that's a strong link, but I doubt he's ever considered me to be a big delight.

I fetched a knife from the kitchen and said, "I'll take those."

I carried the squirrels into the sunny side yard, squatted, and cut away. I needed to hide my feelings, this sense of being slighted, left out of the sincere Panda hugs. I'd rather clean almost anything than squirrels. Rabbits are easy, you can nearly clean them with sharp fingernails, they peel so readily. Quail are a bit of trouble, but they fry up so incredibly tasty. Pheasant could be twice as much trouble and still worth it, their breast meat providing such fine dining. Squirrels are a job, then you have to eat them, and I don't find their taste to be all that delicious. Their skin comes off slow, you have to pull and cut, pull and cut, and as the meat is revealed it's impossible not to think of rat. Soaked in buttermilk overnight they get better, as the buttermilk leaches the tart acorn flavor, I guess, but these particular squirrels weren't destined for a buttermilk bath.

The guts and skin went into the garbage bucket, then I laid the lunch entrées on the porch step. I sat and smoked. From the kitchen I heard the sounds of cold drinks being poured and warm words spoken.

Down the road a ways I could see two boys from that rental shack down there, kneeling on the black road with butter knives. They were happily lancing the tar boils the heat had raised. Both boys had a look I knew so well, and the shack they came from I came from, too. We'd lived there nearly four years after General Jo's parole came through. Such shacks pock our region, hatching batches of children the regular world will have to deal with down the line. These wild kids are reared on baloney and navy beans, corn mush and Kool-Aid, and quick, terrible rough stuff. Their lips are circled by orange or red or green juice stains and their knees and elbows generally have scabs on them from two or three scraps at recess. All they ever know is that they want, and someday they'll learn *you* got, and after that the rest is sirens and statistics and nods from the wall of dead.

Perhaps one of those butter knife–wielding boys will love to read, and he'll read his way beyond the obvious path, or maybe he can hit a baseball four hundred feet, but likely he'll just learn to tolerate his lot in life.

I went inside, dropped the meat in the sink, and turned on the faucet. A glass of Johnnie Red, the ice cubes melted down to thumbnail size, sat on the counter.

"There's your drink," Smoke said.

The scotch scratched the itch. I sipped and watched as Smoke chopped potatoes and Panda ladled grease into two black skillets. The grease came from an old Folger's can, just like the can Mom kept under our sink all my life. The grease had been rendered from the gamut of meats. Bacon grease, pork fat, burger leavings, whatever. It all went into the bucket and mingled, and this mystery grease did wonders. The best fried potatoes or quail or catfish or onions you've ever had sizzled in this grease cooked from a United Nations of edible critters. Looking directly into the mingled-grease bucket should be avoided by the sensitive, but, voilà, the flavor it gave to everything!

I was pouring myself a second Johnnie Red when Panda said, "Your wife called."

"Lizbeth called here?"

"She guessed you might show up." Panda quartered the squirrels with a cleaver, rolled them through a pan of flour, and dropped them into the skillet. The grease popped like wild applause. "I told her you hadn't."

"Good."

"She didn't believe me, Doyle. I lied the best I could, which is damned good, but she never swallowed it. She said to tell you that if she don't get her car back in three days, she's gonna start burnin' your old notebooks and manu-whatnots."

I got a third scotch, quick.

"She wouldn't," I said, though I knew she might.

"For every day you're late, she'll burn another armful."

Smoke laughed, not seeing my side of this at all.

"I don't have copies," I said, anguished.

They both laughed, and I felt left out again, excluded by virtue of outside interests they didn't, couldn't, share or appreciate.

I sat at the table and moped about my apprenticeship scrawlings being burned, wondering how future biographers could get the total picture of my creative development without them, until the fried potatoes and squirrel were served. It's a meal that's not on many restaurant menus, not even à la carte, but it could be if the chef had access to our bucket of mingled grease. The potatoes acquire six flavors at least, all of them good. They don't even want for ketchup. But the true wonder of the grease is such that the gamey squirrel meat has become succulent, so much so it puts the surviving cemetery squirrels on the hit list. The meat is traced with thin, light bones that will bring rat once more to mind if you let them, but the squirrel now rips between your teeth to give a splendid, greasy flavor.

I was gnawing on the last bone when Smoke said, "Panda, I feel I should warn you—Doyle killed him a Dolly last night."

"Doyle? Bullshit."

"No. He did. We buried him way yonder."

Panda undid a cigar, stuck it in his mouth but didn't light it. He was looking at me real steady, watchful, with a new respect or something.

"He need killin'?"

"Oh, yeah," I said. "He needed it. His name was Bunk, Bunk Dolly."

"I've heard of him." Panda lit his cigar, puffed and sighed. "We ain't got the money for killin' Dollys no more, boys. You have to get away with it clean. The cash just ain't there no more."

"We know," I said.

"I believe we'll get away with it," Smoke chipped in. "He's buried pretty good."

Panda stood and walked toward the kitchen window. His big limp seemed bigger, his shuffle tired. Cigar smoke hung around his head, and his shoulders had a slump I'd nevcr noticed before.

"Aw, boys," he said, his back to us, his eyes trained on the cemetery below the house. He was a close, dark outline again, leaning on the sink. "It just seems that every time a Redmond kills a Dolly, why, something bad happens."

16

Rocky Drop

The cliff had been formed by volcanic rock, a stream trickling down its gray face, and Niagra was first to leap from it. She stood poised on the edge of rock, in cutoffs and a T-shirt, staring at the clear and alluring pool of water below.

"Make a wish!" she shouted, then pushed away from the cliff and into the air.

In the air Niagra had center stage. A couple of families with a crowd of children were clustered at the far edge of the pool. They all turned to watch her from there, as we did from the cliff known as Rocky Drop. The drop was eighteen or twenty feet, and Niagra attempted a full forward tumble in the air, but as she righted herself her T-shirt billowed up to her face and she made an innocent, bare-breasted entry into the water.

We cheered, especially me, as it was my first actual viewing of her breasts. The families clapped, the husbands more heartily than the children, the wives rather sullenly. From our perch we could see Niagra in the clear water, slicing to the stony floor of the pool below the drop, or falls. Her hair fanned out and the sunlight caught it, giving a dreamy luminescence to her submerged form.

When her head rose above the surface she went, "Oops!" Then she backstroked, looking at me. "Make a wish, Doyle, and come on down!"

My wish was too obvious to require mention. I stood at the edge, a pair of Smoke's shorts held wadded around my hips by a cinched length of rope. For my dive I selected the classic swan, but I overarched my torso, lost control straightaway, and hit the surface in a spastic, butt-first flop.

I swam to Niagra, who said, "What was that?"

"Death of a swan," I said. "It's my best dive."

The pool at Rocky Drop is near a mountain crest and miles off any paved road, hard to get to. Trees grow near the waterline and tower protectively around three sides of the pool. Rocky Drop looms at the other end, a series of gray boulders and ancient lava slabs where the ripples the cooling lava made are yet visible. The climb to the cliff requires several minutes of delicate stepping and occasional bounds up the volcanic slabs and from boulder to boulder. A few resolute shrubs grow among the rocks and offer roots for handholds.

Niagra put her arms around my neck from behind and clung buoyantly to my back. We watched Smoke and Big Annie smooch hot and funny on the cliff, then down they came. Theirs was a sort of Butch-and-Sundance plummet. Big Annie held her T-shirt in place, and Smoke crouched into a massive cannonball. The whopping splash they made caused the little kids to laugh, though no one else clapped.

Damned Spot was over in the shallows, getting her ankles wet, lapping cool drinks. I'd insisted the dog come along, as her scent had gone high in the heat and a long swim might rinse her down to a ho-hum level of dog-stink.

The water was a delight, clear and clean, with occasional fish on view along the rock bottom. Old tennis shoes, which we all wore, made for perfect comfort. Down home, old tennis shoes should always be retained for canoeing and swimming purposes. Every flow of water has a stone lining in the Ozarks, and you never know when you'll have the urge to dive in someplace, so it's best to keep a pair or two of otherwise useless shoes in the trunk. Water, I'd say, is the major compensation nature blessed our region with. Most of the streams and rivers run clear and pretty, often spring fed and clean enough for trout, even, let alone the more hardy fish. This runoff eventually fills a string of huge and magnificent lakes along the Missouri-Arkansas border, the Lake District. Norfork, Bull Shoals, Table Rock, and Beaver. All this fine water makes up for a lot in terms of cultural deprivation, especially in summer, and I'd rather float down the Current River in an inner tube than sit through a show of modern dance or opera anytime, anyway. The two operas I'd been dragged to by Lizbeth had been way too much like acid flashbacks for me to truly enjoy. I'd eventually been swept over by a kind of narcissistic terror, a sixth sense that the Latin dandies with the long knives and the puffy shirts were hollering about me, somehow.

But down here we've got the water, and banjos and

fiddles and sly-fox storytellers around the square, and not much else.

The gang of us splashed about the pool, committing the standard acts of water mischief: underwater pinches, accidental glimpses of mams, quick little bites, hidden rubs, and surprise splashes to the face. Kid stuff that never dies. You dive into water anywhere at any age and pretty soon your acts will jibe with a sassy eleven-year-old.

I went after Damned Spot during a lull in the playpen. I sat at the water's edge, called her over, and tossed her out a few feet so she'd get wet. She swam back to me, grinning a loose-jaw mutt grin. Next time I carried her out about twenty feet and released her. Her dog paddle to shore looked to be a pretty vigorous washing motion. The thing about dogs is they're not people, so there's never any cause to abuse them, even if they smell or yowl. In California I was popped by the law for knocking tar out of a neighbor fella who'd been beating his animal, a handsome young shepherd with a bark habit, with a tree limb thicker'n my wrist. The man put up a fair scrap 'til I got a thumb in his eye, then I learned him several things about hurt. He dropped charges the next day and apologized to me and moved away within the month, though he stayed on faculty at Hichens College. Dogs don't ever call for that kind of bad treatment, or that's what's in my heart, and I reckon it goes back to grade school and our heinz mutt, Sentry.

I can't talk about Sentry without blubbering to this day. It occurs to me sometimes that Sentry was paid back to the eternal for something Imaru pulled and got away with. That's a line of thought I'd rather shake off and forget, though, so there.

Smoke and Big Annie had floated over to where the green reeds grow, and I could see his big hands were under her wet shirt but I couldn't spot hers. The couples were diligently steering their kids' eyes away from the reeds, pointing up Rocky Drop to watch Niagra climb to the cliff once more.

The way she climbed, with the surefooted grace of a native Ozarker born to hills and hardship and rough pleasure, made my chest swell. Her legs had hillbilly muscles and her swift steps amounted to a prance. The soaking of her garments had resulted in a smashing outline. The wet duds were sealed on her like gift wrap. I could see her nipples from the bank, where I sat cupping clean water over Damned Spot's neck.

I glanced at the crowd watching her ascent and it was pure star appeal at work.

Watching her be so raptly watched, it occurred to me that there were longer shots than Niagra who had made it in pictures. Dick Powell came from across the Arkansas line at Mountain View, and Tess Harper from close by there, too. Sheilah Medley, star of several B flicks and a spy-oriented TV series, had been reared out at Daphne Spring, only seven miles from the West Table square. The blond gal from *The Beverly Hillbillies* lived about a three-beer drive north at Rolla. Anything can happen from anywhere. Niagra had the piss and vinegar to maybe accomplish more than I suspected. She wanted to take her pout and strut and bottle-blond beauty and merge it with the undying style of certain celluloid icons. Take her interior weirdness and nurture it until a singular art bloomed from the fertile warp. But the key to it all was her looks, which might alone ease open a few Wilshire Boulevard doors to her lifetime plans.

At the Rocky Drop cliff she paused to tease her audience. She crouched to stretch the muscles of her legs, ass toward water, then stood and raised her arms and heaved her chest with big sucks of air. All eyes on her, she posed on the rock. She waved to me and Damned Spot and said, "For you, baby."

Her dive met the standards of poetics: style, form, execution, and significance. She sprang way out from the cliff, as in a lover's leap, spun once, briefly assumed the swan, then entered the water like a drop, making hardly a splash except with the crowd.

17

Spot the Silicone

For supper we grilled burgers on the deck, as the house was too hotted up to sit in. By dusk the window fans had blown the heat yonder, and the cooler evening air allowed for sitting inside, with only light sweating. The whole gang sat in front of the tube to watch videos the ladies had rented off the one-dollar rack at Pritchard's on the square.

I fetched ice in a plastic bag for Niagra, who'd banged her head on the bottom rocks with her last beautiful dive at Rocky Drop. She had a bruise and a slight break in the skin near the hairline above her forehead. She sat on the couch, near the fan, and held the bag in place.

The flick was something silly, but it took place on a gorgeous beach somewhere in the beach-bearing portion of our nation. Some dweeb had inherited a Coney Dog stand near a boardwalk, and he and the other youngsters hit on the notion of using female pulchritude to market weenies. The gals involved as a sales force donned thongs and frequently less when a big sales day led to sandy frolics of success as the sun set.

It was watchable.

During the plot development scenes, when the banker threatens to foreclose if he doesn't get a balloon payment by Friday, and the rich Arab oil-ghoul tries to buy the dweeb out because he reckons as owner he'd get to despoil the sales force, my thoughts wandered. A new book was starting to talk to me, and it wasn't about The Hyena, but Imaru. A long novel of Imaru, and when we harvested that money garden I'd be in the position to take the time and write it. The opening was finding shape as a scene of the Big Bang, Imaru as an atom, a speck, then a newt. Yeah, it'd surely be the longest novel I'd written, by far.

"Those ain't real!" Niagra said. She took the ice from her head and sat forward. "Fakers!"

"No shit, hon," Big Annie said. "Those there are factory titties."

"The lack of sincerity!"

"I know big tits, and they don't behave like that."

"Fake tits, fake faces—fake acting!"

The gals on screen did have breasts that displayed a haughty indifference to the laws of gravity. Thirty-eight D's that don't wobble or droop, real feats of bosom engineering.

"So what," Smoke said as he lit a doobie. "Less I'm silly I believe these babes are gonna carry the day for the weenie stand."

But Niagra had a total investment of dreams in that nineteen-inch screen, and had standards of expectation. Truly, I believe she wanted to live there, in the tube, on a screen that was smaller than actual life but so much nearer

111

to rapture in terms of scenery and plot potential. Feature films would rate even better, as then even her nostrils would be larger than a filled seat in the audience.

"See here," Big Annie said. She left her chair. "Watch my tits." She settled to the floor, laid on her back, and her breasts dove toward her armpits like rabbits into holes. "These mamas are real—and that's how they really behave!"

"Co-rrect," Niagra said. Her face had flushed pink from sunshine and indignation. I could see she actually was angry at those thespians who'd opted for implants. "It's fuckin' disgustin'!"

In her anger and use of foul language, Niagra was still endearing, like an angel telling fart jokes.

I tried to help.

"Those, there, the gal in blue, those are silicone."

The whole flick got critiqued as to the use of breasts as mise-en-scène. The ladies came up with rather harsh denunciations. Occasionally an actress rated a grudging "Well, maybe. Hard to tell about those."

Smoke found the aesthetic arguments put forth by the ladies to be vengeful, moot, hot air.

"Hooters is hooters. Christ!"

His comment failed to extinguish the discussion of the real versus the fake. This concern had much larger dimensions to it than just breasts, and I vowed to myself not to ever be phony with Niagra if I could help it.

I guess I was the only one who heard the car door slam. The flick had reached the happy finale, the banker was eating crow, the Arab was under arrest for fraud, and the dweeb had matured into a mere nerd and found true love.

I looked out the window, then calmly said, "A Chevy full of strangers just pulled in."

Smoke jumped up, peeked out.

Damned Spot had started barking.

"Where's your pistol?"

"On the shelf."

"Put it in your belt, baby bro. That's Roy Don Springer and what looks to be a few Dollys."

"If they ain't Dollys," I said, "they're Dolly imitators."

"What is that they're carryin'?"

18

Hey, Neighbor

"Meat," Springer said. He gestured at one of the two surly thug-puppy Dollys who accompanied him, the one carrying a foil-wrapped object. "Venison. Twitchin' fresh."

"Poached her today, huh," Smoke said.

"No, no—not poached," Springer said. He was pushing fifty, I'd guess, with red skin, a permanent flush. I recognized him from round and about, though I'd never known his name. The male pattern problem had worked over his head, and what hair he had left was long, uncombed, and black. He stood near five ten, thick limbed, with a pony keg of beer for a gut. His stag-cut shirt had blood smears on the chest and his jeans looked stained along the thighs, and these duds were all wrinkled and drooping and seemed to be straining to cling on to him. "This doe here, she had a accident, just one of those things."

"Of course," Smoke said. He was acting cordial but his

eyes were watchful. "You were test-firin' at a barn door or somethin'—"

"Right, right. That's the story. Just a test shot at a apple tree, but out she sprang from nowhere, leaped right into the slug."

"An emotionally stressed doe," Smoke said. "Clearly suicide."

"That's it," Springer said, an exemplar of the shit-eatin' grin on his face. "That's surely the way it happened, Mr. Smoke." The thug puppies murmured their amusement, and the one female in the group shyly lowered her face. "Only you know them pissant laws—they don't understand how nature truly is."

"There's lots of deer suicides," I said. "Especially out of season."

"They're high-strung that way, sure 'nough." He gestured at the package. "Ed, hand that meat over to Miss Annie, there."

When Big Annie accepted the package, she said, "You'd like to have us eat some evidence for you, would you?"

"Sure would, Miss Annie," Springer said. Then he gestured at his entourage. "These are my cousins, Ed Dolly, there, and Milton Dolly over here." Ed and Milton aped Springer's dress in every particular, including the ill-fitting clothes. They were in their early twenties and wore their hair about like Elvis, only instead of ducktails they had manes that flopped to midback. A home dye-job had been done on both of them so they had the jet-black locks of The King. Their eyebrows were blond still, imparting a two-tone, forest-creature aspect to their looks. "And this is my woman, Shareena."

Shareena said a cautious "Hey." Ozarker women who

had men the breed of Springer tended to avoid eye contact with other men, especially strangers. If possible, when meeting strange men these gals would stand back until they just blended into the draperies. Shareena was scarce-hipped, with short brown hair, and looked to have lived about thirty-three rough and frightened years.

"Too bad we've eaten," Niagra said. She was in the kitchen, behind me and Smoke, leaning on the fridge. There wasn't much welcome in her body language, but she flashed a showstopper smile. "Not long ago, either."

"Now that is too bad, Miss Niagra." Springer was one of those down-home types that affects a faux courtly style, so overly respectful in manner as to signify no respect at all. He then turned to me, hand out. "Haven't had the pleasure, sir—you'd be?"

"I'd be the Nobel Prize winner," I said, "if I could. But so far I'm just ol' Doyle Redmond."

I shook his hand, and he surveyed me pretty thoroughly.

"Roy Don Springer, sir."

"Charmed," I said.

"Ah. Another of Mr. Panda's kids, are you?"

"Grandson."

"If you say so, Mr. Doyle."

The thug puppies eased back onto the deck and drifted out of sight. They looked like the sort of fellas who might spend their idle hours dropping thumbtacks on beaches. I tried to see them over Springer's shoulder, but I couldn't.

"Let's have a beer," I said. Niagra gave me a sour glance at that. "It's hot. A couple of cold ones on the deck."

"I've got some rum in the car," Springer said. "Shareena, how about gettin' it?"

"Huh—no," Shareena said. "Not that one-fifty-one rum."

"Beer's fine," Smoke said. "We've got plenty."

"That one-fifty-one," Shareena said, her glance averted from her man, "it stirs up crazy stuff."

Springer took a sudden step toward Shareena and she flinched, but before he could raise a hand to her Big Annie shoved a beer can at him. He took it, popped the tab.

"Beer it is," he said. He raised the can. "To all the lovely ladies," he toasted, then had a loud slurp.

A few beers down the line, we males stood on the deck, swatting mosquitoes, doing a sort of talk-talk macho sparring, each of us subtly implying that we were secretly ultradangerous dudes who ought not be fucked with by less than a regiment. I'd say Springer was winning on points, as his innuendos and veiled boasts had the flavor of fact, whereas Smoke and me's came across as mere warnings.

The thug puppies sat under a tree, away from the deck, sharing a tiny pipe of herb, petting Damned Spot. They'd been all over the grounds, down to the barn, around the house, skulking here and there, claiming they had to take leaks.

That ladystinger in my belt felt sweet to me.

I stayed in front of Springer the whole time. The man had the fingernail on his pinkie grown out an inch or better into a permanent coke spoon accoutrement. I hadn't seen many fingernail coke spoons for some time, as others who'd sported them had munched them down to the bloody quick in detox years ago. But this tush hog, Springer, stuck with the fashion of his younger manhood,

I suppose. I couldn't imagine me, for instance, wearing a roach-clip necklace or a Grand Funk Railroad T-shirt ever again, but this cat had found a groove he never wanted to leave.

The females were in the kitchen, sitting at the table, playing Trivial Pursuit. Country folk love their board games, the kind that can eat up a whole evening and be called entertainment.

Springer had fetched the one-fifty-one rum himself. I held a brew, Smoke, too, and Springer held the rum in one fist and a beer in the other. Peepers and crickets had set up a constant racket, like an edgy soundtrack to our socializing.

Springer said, for some reason, "Pipe bombs really are simple, you unnerstan'? They only take a few minutes to patch together."

"I wouldn't know," I said.

"They make nice booms."

"Seems like it'd take more'n a few minutes."

"The boom impresses whoever hears it."

"To do it right, seems like it'd take more'n a few minutes."

"But C-4, that's what I wish I had."

"That's serious stuff, C-4."

"You bet it is. It'll blast a hole in somebody's front yard so deep they won't never testify."

"I'd guess that's right."

"I could use about a case of it," he said. "They're callin' another grand jury, I reckon."

Smoke said, "I hadn't heard that."

"Well, I have." The man was well along to drunk.

"Them laws—they think we do everything. Dollys, you know. My mom's a Dolly, and that's it to these laws round here—I must be guilty of somethin'." He staggered a little stagger. "Or everything."

"Boo-hoo," I went, and Smoke laughed, but he nudged me and gave me a kind of "Be cool, bro" look.

"Huh?"

"That they do," I said.

"Yeah, Mr. Doyle. That could be what you said. It ain't what I *heard,* but . . ."

The ladies began to loudly fuss over something in the kitchen. We all glanced that way. They weren't mad so much as excited. Big Annie stood next to the screen door and called for Smoke.

"Smoke, come here." She turned back to the other contestants and said, "He'll know." As Smoke approached the door she asked, " 'The Galloping Ghost,' that was a white guy, wasn't it? Not Jim Brown."

I heard Smoke chuckle, then he went inside to referee.

He said something along the lines of, That dude was way back, back when there *were* white running backs.

"Pussy at play," Springer said. "Gives me raunchy thoughts."

He thought he was funny, thought I wouldn't mind him molesting our women in his mind. I had begun to resent his slovenly swagger, his confidence that he was the apex predator, straw boss of the food chain.

"You ever fuck a woman wasn't scared of you?" I asked. "Or shit-faced drunk?"

He gave me his number-one killer look, a slit-eyed, impervious stare.

"Just your mama," he said. At my silence, he gave me a li'l shove. "Now, go on and laugh, Mr. Doyle, we's just a couple of fellers, funnin' around."

In therapy, the straight therapy I'd gone through before entering regression therapy and discovering Imaru, I'd recounted my memories of life in pathetic detail. The lady therapist who was interpreting my history back at me said that one constant seemed to be a need in me to confront or fight both institutions of society and individuals where I had slim or no chance of victory. That my raising had planted in me a need to stand sullen and defiant, especially against those forces that could crush me like a Bass Weejun on a nightcrawler.

This trait is a frequent pain producer but, by God, it keeps life simmering.

I never learned why I'm that way, but I sort of knew why I thought of that, out on the deck, schmoozing with Springer.

"I'll let it pass," I said.

"Is that right? Mighty big of you. You'll let it pass." Springer gave a heavy, slow shake of his head. "You know who I am?"

I fired a Lucky, then said, "I reckon."

"No, you don't, Mr. Doyle, Mr. Doyle Redmond. You'll let it pass—*that's* fuckin' funny. I mean, *you'll* let a li'l joke pass, but settin' right over there is Ed and Milton, who is grandkids to a feller named Logan, who your Mr. Panda murdered, stone cold."

"He paid what the Dollys said Logan was worth."

"Uh-huh. Logan was my uncle, you know."

"I didn't know."

"I'll let *that* pass," he said. "Logan"—he began to wave

that bottle of one-fifty-one around—"I understand from our people, and a couple of recollections of my own, that he was a man of ideas. Couldn't seem to keep 'em to himself when he had one, neither. He was good at numbers, could count up to nine, anyhow. That give him one of his ideas he couldn't keep to himself. The idea he got, because he could count to nine, see, was that Mr. Panda might could be Mr. Smoke's daddy."

I just stood there, inhaling.

He went on.

"The man you call Daddy, see, the way I had it run down to me, you know, he was in Korea or some gook spot for quite a few months more than nine, whilst your mama lived with Mr. Panda, the seed bull, you see, over by the . . ."

My first punch, a left hook, caught him high on the skull, as he'd sensed the blow's route and turned just that much. He grunted, came around with that one-fifty-one bottle, and I jammed him hard near his wrist and the bottle came loose, caught me on the ear. I grabbed him inside both elbows, stubbing my Lucky on his flesh, and he splashed beer toward my eyes, so I lowered my face and butted him, jumping the hard part of my forehead against his nose. I felt it give. There was a sound, a piffle, sort of, and he went "Uh!" This brought his hands up some, the pain, you know, and I snapped a strong knee into his manhood package. My ear felt swollen, maybe gone. I brought my left arm up, cocked the elbow, pivoted fast and beat him in the face with that sharp bone like a cudgel, time and again.

I said something along the lines of, "You wife-beatin' sack of shit."

He went down—he was only human. I had just planted one solid kick in on him around the beltline when the thug puppies came hurdling over the deck rail.

Damned Spot got all frenzied and baffled, not sure if she was expected to sink fangs into those who'd so recently petted her.

Milton and Ed both had blades out pretty quick, Buck knives, but they squared up in front of me and hesitated instead of shanking me before I could pull my sweet ladystinger.

They stared at that pistol, a big Huh? expression on both their weird faces.

The screen door opened, I heard that, and the thug puppies started to close in with those blades, ladystinger or no ladystinger, coming as they did from a bloodline noted for engendering in its members a rare sort of invincible stupidity.

I was only two finger jerks away from becoming a mass murderer, when, *wham!* Smoke belted one of them from behind (Milton, I'm gonna guess), then the other turned and caught a big Smoke fist flush on his chin.

Boy howdy, Smoke had gone through them two knife-wielding Dollys faster'n hot sauce through a widow woman! Those thug puppies were both down and out, as unconscious as toddlers who'd mistook mommie's flask of Old Crow for Co-Cola.

"Doyle, man, what the fuck is with you?"

"He bothered me."

"He what? He *bothered* you? Jesus, baby bro, he'll backshoot you now—that'll *really* bother you."

The trio of women came onto the deck. They weren't in a talking mood. They just stood there, watching Damned

Spot sniff around the flattened Dollys. Springer had begun to make a bit of noise, sputters and moans, that sort of thing.

"I enjoyed the game," Shareena said to Niagra and Big Annie. "I learned some answers." Then she walked to the site of the fight. "I reckon I better carry the menfolk on home right quick. They'll come to and be mad, don't you know."

"We'll drag 'em to your car," Smoke said. "Give you a hand. I want you to know we don't have a thing in the world against you, Shareena."

"I understand how it is," Shareena said. "It's just that one-fifty-one rum, it leads to bad stuff every time. My mister, he can't live without it, though it makes him awful crazy. Course it don't make him near as crazy as you peckerwoods is, if you ain't got sense enough to shoot the whole three of them Dollys this very minute."

The dust from the departing Chevy had settled. The gang stood around in the kitchen, not saying much. Smoke kept looking at me and shaking his head. I'd had the normal postscrap case of frantic butterflies, but now the scared was out of me. Finally Smoke's constant but unasked questions forced me to a response: "Old sins cast long shadows."

Big bro merely stared.

Niagra pulled the venison from the fridge, slapped it on the counter. She unwrapped the foil and revealed a mound of red doe steaks.

"We ain't eatin' this poor girl," she said. "I suspect this meat." She shuffled the steaks with delicately pinched fingers. "We best not even feed it to Damned Spot."

19

For Real-ism

The moon had gotten blood on its face. There was some wind kicking up in the night, a hint of fractious weather on the way. The tall trees wobbled in sudden stops and starts, like paranoid druggies, their leaves speed-rappin' nonsensical prattle. Yet the sky was spread wide and clear, in sharp focus, no clouds at all visible in the frame. The money garden swayed beneath the red moon, too, the individual plants spread about us, standing mute, as a stoic tribe might, each somber stalk occasionally nodding in grim approval.

We were on guard, Niagra sitting cross-legged with a shotgun splayed across her lap, me packing the ladystinger. I didn't believe we could be ripped off this night, as the Dollys were busted up pretty sore. But Smoke and Big Annie weren't so sanguine of that, so there we sat, posted in the deep woods to oversee the financial flora, protect the blue-chip greenery. On the slim chance that patch bandits might tail us, we'd parked the Volvo at Panda's, then snuck through the cemetery, past Tararum and into the woods.

I had pulled Niagra's boots off and now held her bare feet in my lap. My ear throbbed and had swelled some, but the main feeling I throbbed with was romantic. She'd brought a roll of clear tape and I applied swatches from it to her ankles and feet. Seed ticks are too small to pluck individually, and if you've got one you've got an army on you. The tape swatches pick them up best, a squad at a time. I sat there, holding her pretty feet, rolling that tape after seed ticks, and hell, man, I knew I was in love.

She knew it, too. She spoke of many things, the casual and the deeply felt. The girl had some dreams that were mighty fleshed out, full of detail, and she spoke of them as nearly factual.

I've always been vulnerable to my own dreams, too. I could relate to the symptoms if not to the exact fever. It seems Niagra read every biography of old Hollywood in paperback, and some of her dream-plans would need updating. I tried to impart current knowledge gently to this kid, who I guess I loved.

She said, "Then, maybe I'll have to get work. Square work. Probably start as a hatcheck girl at The Mocambo, I imagine."

"I believe The Mocambo is gone," I said.

"Since when?"

"Oh, I guess twenty or thirty years ago."

"No! Shit." Her feet squirmed in my lap. "So, it'll have to be Ciro's, then."

I didn't have the heart.

I let Ciro's still exist.

The night wind goosed my mood, gusting along with summertime warmth. The temperature was at that exact, fabulous level where body heat and air are on a par and there's a weightless sense, an overwhelming oneness with the atmosphere. Hardy amounts of sweat, but still the feeling of a godly cuddle out there amidst the smell of the forest and the creek and a hillbilly girl's feet in August.

Niagra talked on. "Now, and surely you must have noticed this, when they belch, you can smell the beer. When they kiss, you can hear heartbeats, sniff the juice, feel the undies waddin'. When they act mean, you just know they were raised up mighty wrong and have to be that way."

I had lost her thread while in revery, but nodded anyway.

"And the thing is, Doyle, they have so much outright for real-ism to their style, why they can convince you of most anything with only a look. A sneer. The way they walk."

"Uh-huh," I said. "Who're these people again?"

"The Method people. A style of actors."

"Well, yeah. Brando, Dean—all those mumbly, twitchy sorts, right?"

"They mumble and twitch to reach a new level of for real-ism." She pulled her feet from my lap, signifying a slight miff, I guess, then curled them beneath her can. "Marilyn Monroe went in for it, too. That movie I'm named for she was the star of. I feel . . . well . . ."

"A connection?"

"That's it." She giggled and looked down. "There might could be somethin' to that."

"You're named for her flick—that's somethin' right there."

"More'n that. I don't want to say out loud what all—but a strong goomer could tap into it."

So there we sat, in the deep woods, armed fairly well, listening to freight trains whistle and clack across the hills, chatting about thespian matters. Niagra had come across a copy of *Strasberg at the Actors Studio* at the Book Nook down in Hardy, Arkansas, and had devoured it. I dropped a couple of complimentary comments about Method acting, mostly drawn from Tennessee Williams's plays on film, and she shoved her bare feet back onto my lap. I flapped jaws about Julie Harris and Gena Rowlands, Al Pacino and Karl Malden.

"Karl Malden?" she said. "Ain't he that tater-nosed fella, wears a hat, sells credit cards on TV?"

"That's him *now*," I said. "But he's famous for bein' Method, you know."

"No," she said, "I didn't. But I guess I mean the Method more of James Dean, Al Pacino—like that."

"The cuter Method ones."

"Are they?" she said. "They're the ones that really send me with those chills of for real-ism, anyhow."

"Those Method actors, though, Niagra, they go into some scary places, emotionally scary, to give out those real-world chills."

"I want to act," she said. "Scary won't much scare me." Her toes wrinkled and flexed and she leaned back, her hands snapping twigs as her weight lowered. "The Method people make whatever they act seem like the real world, and that's the only scary place I know of."

"The real world?"

"Where the real world meets me—that's the scary place."

Along in there I was doing my best to ape a teenager in love. I'd never had one of those teenage heartbreaks the teenage years are so noted for. No lost love from my seventeenth year haunts me, and I suppose I feel a bit cheated by that. I hadn't yet become too comfortable with decent girls before I hit the Marine Corps, and at Camp Pendleton I became comfortable with the wrong sort of girls, mainly from down along the Mexican border, most of them in the fifteen- to twenty-dollar range. It was my seventeenth year and all, but none of those quick pokes in whorehouse cribs were so true-blue or emotional as to haunt. Though there was a skinny li'l gal who chewed an orange while I flailed my manhood to and fro inside her, her jaws mashing hard on those orange wedges so that the juice splattered my eyes, the acidity causing them to well. She seemed starved for fruit. That's an intimate moment I don't imagine I'll ever forget, but not because any high, wondrous emotions were involved.

So, stolen kisses in the school hallway between classes, prom night seduction, all that sort of young romance activity, was fresh to me. Smooching at the Dog'N Suds, my class ring worn on a string around a girl's neck, parents who just didn't understand—I'd never been there. Now here I was, having a sort of teenage love affair, only I was thirty-five years old having it, and hear this clear—it was everything common legend had glossed it up to be, and more.

But full of hidden shoals.

Niagra said: "I guess it's big-headed, but I believe that

somehow I am just, I don't know—*so much extra.* There's more to me than most. That's why I'll meet up with Mr. Lee Strasberg, make him be my guide, my teacher, until I have full powers."

"Well," I said. "It doesn't have to be Lee Strasberg."

"Yes, it does. He has a West Coast Actors Studio, too."

"There's plenty of teachers of the Method. A lot of them would probably do."

"Uh-uh. It'll be Lee Strasberg his own self for me."

"That won't work," I said. "Niagra, ol' Strasberg is dead."

Her face drained, went slack-jawed and deflated.

"Don't say that, Doyle. It's not funny."

"Kid—he passed several years ago."

"No!"

"Eighty-two, -three, in there."

As she began to believe me, she began to weep. I'd caused my hillbillyette beauty to cry by waylaying her with unwanted knowledge. She fell back on the dirt and leaves and twigs, sobbing. She said, "So, it's more tough titty to me, huh?"

One leg of her dream had withered, and not a word would be said for over an hour. I rubbed her bare feet, avoiding any urge to offer comment, watching her shoulders shake as she wept tears for Lee Strasberg into her clenched fists.

20

Shooky Bizness

Niagra and me followed the young-love urge, holding hands as we picked our way through the woods. A burgeoning courtliness compelled me to carry her shotgun loosely at my side, the ladystinger riding in a back pocket. Trees and shrubs and sudden gullies forced our hands apart now and then, until we reached the clear-cut lawn of Tararum. It was the hour before dawn and the air blew cool. The drumstick palace loomed lightless and Gothic, and we took advantage of the privacy the time of night afforded to sidle alongside the sexy yard statues and grope them.

Whichever of the Byrums had chosen the statues had clearly swooned for the ancients, as all the human forms seemed to aspire to an ancient Greekness in anatomical ideology. The females had smallish breasts and pitchers or platters in their hands, and the males were curly-haired bucks with impeccable butts. Niagra placed her hands on one such rump, the intensity of her groping indicating her fondness for the artsy, cheap thrill of it all.

She stared at Tararum and said, "These mansion folks, they live these lives where *all* the accessories are at hand."

"This *should* be our land still."

"I've got to tell you something, Doyle," she said. Her fingers slid all over that Greek dude's classic butt. "I'm truly quotin' my feelings here—I need to be fucked."

Those words, long awaited, hit me like happy slaps.

There are acres of tombstones, headstones, and small metal crosses spread across the cemetery, and I led her by the hand, walking without clear thought but directly to the section where Redmonds are planted. Two knobby oak trees overhang the prime family plot, and the headstone inscriptions put names to many faces from the wall of dead. Several of the graves have sunk into the earth, leaving depressions of the shape and size common to soft mattresses long slept on.

"Here?" I asked.

"Good as any."

The sky had begun to pearl, the sun's arrival but a small twist of the globe away. The grass was cut short and slathered with dew. A pickup truck hacked slowly to life somewhere nearby, then began to roar.

Niagra assumed a stance, looked at the graves, then slid her shorts down, pulling them around her red boots, then stepping free. She wore bright white panties, panties of the everyday, innocent sort, and the boots rode high on her calves. Her expression was studious, sincere, as she walked among the headstones, tapping her fingers to each one.

"Any of these special?" she asked.

I pondered the question, the pearly light allowing me to read the Redmond names: Isaac, Thomas, John W., Permelia and child, Aquilla, devoted father, Charlotte, baby Louisa, another Thomas, another Aquilla, baby Earl, Jeb, Manfred, Regina, then Doyle. Sun-bleached bouquets of plastic flowers had gotten scattered among the graves, the cup stands blown over, the fake blooms rearranged by the breeze and the casual kicks of kids playing games of war and revenge in the natural playground afforded by these acres of dead.

I couldn't say no to Doyle. Doyle had a rounded headstone, perhaps three feet tall. Doyle lived rough, and Doyle died young.

Imaru likes him.

"I reckon he'd be good for a goomer."

I leaned the shotgun against an Aquilla, the devoted father. I saw Niagra clear enough, the red boots, white panties, strong legs.

"Your top," I said. "Take it off."

Her eyes, those green eyes, so smart and sleepy, were hidden from me, but her shoulders fluttered in a shrug.

"I reckon that's the way," she said. She slid her fingers beneath the straps to yank off the top, then said, "You let your ponytail loose, too. Like a wild man. A goomer doctor."

Done. My long dark hair flew forward, tangled, and her top whisked up, then dropped to the dew. She posed there in red boots and clean white panties, her hands at her side, one knee cocked at an angle, arched above a narrow red toe stabbed into the dirt, heel raised, a shitkicker pointe. She smiled serenely, confident of her effect, then placed her hands to her breasts and lightly brushed the nipples until they ripened like berries.

"I know you know," I said, "that you're gorgeous."

"Oh, yeah, I know." Niagra then dropped her hands to her waist, crouched, and slithered the schoolgirl panties off over her boots, the entire movement executed with a frolicsome grace that promised rhythm and force and lubricious delight. "We've got to beat dawn," she said, then tossed the undies to the wet grass. "I'd like this to be private—so get naked."

My clothes were shed like they were aflame, boots tossed here, shirt there, jeans wherever the kick took them to. In the pearly light Niagra's blond hair approached radiance, beckoning, and the word "gossamer" perched on the tip of my tongue.

"That looks sort of big," she said.

"Well," I said—then a pathetic honesty got a grip on me, and I heard myself blurt the sort of fact a teenage boy tends to feverishly research, then dwell on—"just about an inch over the national average."

She nodded slowly.

"Proud to know it."

I made a move toward her, arms wide, about to embark on the preliminary touches, an array of lips and tongue and fingertips, courtly foreplay to reassure a novice. But this virgin would have none of that: she scanned the sky, saw the yellow rim to the east. I'd sunk to my knees, thinking to demonstrate phase two of my oral technique, but she pushed my head back.

"No time," she said. "My twitchet'd be sour, any-how—sittin' in the woods all night, peein' behind trees and everything."

Niagra spit on the fingers of her right hand, then massaged saliva into her twitchet. She bent over Doyle, the 1923–1947 He Rests In His Arms Now Doyle, belly to the headstone, ass up.

"Do me this way—they say it's the most potent for goomers."

She had happily assumed a coital position I never object to. I approached, noting the taper of her back from broad shoulders to narrow waist, the striations of muscle, trapezius, I think, and the way in which her ass was defined separately from her thighs, not all of one piece, the butt firm and round and succulent. Then a quick scoot up, bare feet squishing in dew, and entry.

"Uhn," she goes. "Uhn."

When the pumping picked up pace, Niagra shook her hair from her eyes and gave me a look over her shoulder. She clutched tightly to the headstone, her hair flying with each stroke. She wore an impatient, gnarled expression.

"Uhn. Uhn."

The sex act was of rude quality. Clearly no orchestra burst into sound in her head, there was no sudden string section serenading such lovers as us to passionate fulfillment. There was me, pumping, not so unhappily, but in a utilitarian spirit, and the Virgin Niagra staring over her shoulder, green eyes wide, lips clinched thin.

"Uhn. Uhn."

My hair whipped wide and tangly, and as I neared the squirt, rubberless and conscious of it, I pulled out and splashed come on her behind and legs, the white drops firing wildly, spattering her from thigh to hair. As the hot drops dropped, Niagra laughed, and quivered, and laughed, until she gasped for air.

I plopped to the ground, lay back, and Niagra stood. She patted her hands to the hot spots, and inspected the semen on her rubbing fingers.

"Aw, shooky!" she said. She held her fingers to her lips, tried a lick, then laughed again. "Shoo-ky!"

The dawn had reached us. Daybreak squirrels chattered in the graveyard trees. I watched Niagra bend to the ground, her red boots slipping on the dew as she retrieved her panties. She used them as a towel, drying her hair, her back, her legs.

"I'll put all this in my 'useful experience' memory bank," she said. "I've got to say it, though—I liked the oral better. But now, at last, I reckon you'n me done the whole shooky bizness."

21

Creamed Corn and Desire

Smoke took them down with a machete slash a couple of feet above the ground. They fell to the side, the branches shuddering, five-point leaves fluttering like hands held up before terror. He slashed away beneath the evening sun, becoming more expert with each swing of the machete.

I followed my big brother, gathering the plants into sheaves of four, then inserting them as far as I could into black plastic bags. A big brother can loom so hugely in the younger brother's eyes, and one such as Smoke takes on legendary and critical import. I watched Smoke work that blade, his shirt off, and a comment of his original ex-wife, Sandra, came to mind. "Honey, the first time I ever saw Smoke was at the Eleven Point River, and I thought, Goodness gracious, *Hercules* has come for a swim!" He'd been eighteen and perfect then, and they'd married within a month of her first thought of him. But it was soon plain that Hercules and domesticity didn't jibe, and Sandra divorced him a year later.

The harvest was a hot bit of itchy work. A lot of hunching low and scrambling under was involved. The heat was still hanging about, even as the sun went yonder, and we both sweated like politicians on Judgment Day. A jug of iced tea sat on the dirt nearby, and we drank straight from the spigot, the cold liquid spilling over our lips and onto our chests and bellies as we quenched our thirsts with a sort of barbaric license.

Part of my job was to look sharp for any buds that might have jangled loose when the blade met the plant. I squatted, duckwalked along the trail of weed, listening to the swoosh and crack of Smoke's machete strokes. It's a strange, powerful, bloodline poetry, I guess, but there's something so potent to us Redmonds about bustin' laws together, as a family. It's hard to say no to it.

Once, when I was twenty-six or so and in Lawrence, Kansas, living briefly with an older lady who tried to control me with her pocketbook and published status, Smoke fell by and said, "I need you to take my back." At the time he lived in K.C., just an easy stagger from Jimmy's Jigger, with a real young girl who went to the art institute. He carried me to K.C. in his big ol' Cutlass and we parked in the Country Club Plaza area. He fronted me a pistol and I stashed it in my coat.

It seems this abstract expressionist girl Smoke was nuts about had gotten to be a fresh young decadent amongst the student art crowd, which was fine, but he'd come home to find her in the arms of concerned neighbors, turning blue of skin behind an intellectual experiment with smack. Smoke had found out where she'd gotten it, so he led us from the Plaza over to Volker Park.

The man in question was a dashingly scuzzy dude, with skin a beguiling shade of junkie pallor, who set up shop near the fountain most days, and feasted on the coeds and outright chicks from both the nearby university and the art institute. Smoke's girlfriend was at that age where needle-and-spoon street life and all seem to the yearning and bold to offer a kind of back-alley route to significant spiritual development.

But Smoke hated smack just one notch less than he did smack dealers.

The dealer wore the cool long black coat and far-out footwear and doper sunglasses that befit his role in life. He sported a porkpie hat and an air of existential danger, as if he saw himself as a mélange of Bogart and Charlie Parker and Pretty Boy Floyd. He landed on his ass, though, already in deep shit before he realized he had a problem. Some sort of cheapskate armament was in his pocket, but Smoke flipped it into the fountain and went to work. He put a few gruesome kicks into the man's body. The fella kept sayin', "What is it? What is it?" Wondering, I reckon, if he was under arrest or just on the spot.

Two or three of the dude's acolytes stood close by, near the treeline, there, but I put the pistol on them and said, "This is only his problem."

They backed off, out of sight, probably jumped an express bus to Prairie Village, but a bunch of strollers and loungers saw the whole thing. Most of them gathered up their works, or picnic blankets, and hustled away, but a few shouted derogatory comments at us.

The dude was a mess in swift order, and glassine smack

squares floated beneath the splashing waters of the fountain. Smoke looked at me once, his knuckles bloody, face a li'l crazy, his mad eyes asking the question, Do you recognize me?

Then he stopped, maybe one ugly skull thump shy of murder.

I went through the man's pockets, found the money roll. I was disappointed in the amount.

"We might as well rob him, too," I said. "Gas money."

The painter girl with the artist's yen for the creative revelations thought to be comprehensible only through degrading experience was soon okay, and furious with Smoke. She moved out on him, but never did snitch to the dealer or the law.

That night, when he dropped me back in Lawrence, he'd said, "Baby bro, don't it seem most everything you'n me do together we have to run from?"

"Yeah. Or deny under oath, at least."

"Uh-huh. Us Redmond boys, we're a good match."

"Now and then," I said. "And always for reasons."

At sunset, cartoon colors riffled across the sky. Big Mama Nature had splashed a gaudy spread of hues at the outer rim of the world. The money garden was all cashed in, stashed in the black plastic bags. We took a rest break before loading the truck, as we couldn't leave until full dark anyway.

Tree toads buzzed, and you could hear gears mashing as trucks hit the hill on the slab highway beyond the woods.

I felt good about most everything. I was champing to get my cut, write another novel. Maybe not one about Imaru after all, as I didn't know him/her real well yet. It could be another Hyena story, *The Hyena Down Home,* something like that. There's this thing about books and me that goes deep, to the core.

As a boy I was often jammed-up for knowing things, things from books I swallowed straight, haunting the public library for more.

Knowledge made me mix poorly. Boys'd be hanging around the stockyard, leaning on the fence, and some peckerwood scholar would venture something like, "Daddy told me China gals got snatches go sideways 'stead of up'n down," or "George Washington lost us the war at Gettysburg," or starts screaming that he's been out of state plenty and knows damned well and for certain that Louisiana is in New Orleans and not the other way around.

At such moments I'd pipe up with some pertinent insight or fact gleaned from the many pages I'd turned, something commonsensical and easily proven, get smacked or spit at, called a bookworm doofus smarty-mouth, fight back the best I could. I didn't truly get my growth until I was in The Corps, so plenty of these anti-intellectual skirmishes were so unfair in terms of size and age that Mom'd make Smoke go and prove my point for me.

But when I hit twelve or thirteen, Smoke, too, after many learned quibbles and snide asides from me, decided that I *was* a bookworm doofus smarty-mouth, and walked all over town saying he would no longer straighten out disputes caused by my incorrigible smart-assedness.

It's a trait he still watches me for signs of.

He got good and even with me once. I was sixteen, and Jack London was to blame. I had long since begun to write my own stories in bed at night, but I needed a role model. Jack London became the one. I read this biography of him, by Irving Stone, I imagine, and found out that by age fifteen Jack had become an oyster pirate with his own boat and a whore who lived on board with him for free! Here I was, already *sixteen,* with no remotely similar romantic experiences behind me I could one day recount—*life was just passing me right by!*

We had only recently moved to K.C., and I decided I should at least become a boxer. I beat the shit out of General Jo's old army duffel bag in the basement. I made the house rattle. I stole every *Ring* magazine from Walgreens and studied.

I got to the point where I thought I knew a thing or two about the manly art, the squared circle.

Smoke was over to supper for his birthday. He was on wife number two then, Ruth Ann the beautician's apprentice. Just before time to eat, Mom said to him, "Put the gloves on with Doyle, Smoke, see if the boy's got anything."

We pulled the gloves on in the basement, a poor prize ring. The walls were bare concrete, and there were shelves of canned goods all over that Mom had bought on special. The ceiling was low enough Smoke had to hunch.

I'd read several articles about Young Griffo, a boxer so smart and scientific he could stand on a hankie and yet couldn't be punched in the face during a three-minute round. I thought, Smart? Scientific? Hell, that's me.

I popped two quick jabs to Smoke's nose, and it reddened encouragingly, and I sensed I was in with a mere brute, an unschooled slugger, hooked once to his liver, and then I remember this train wreck in my head, and all these cans of creamed corn were raining on my face. I didn't duck hardly any—the cans landed.

"Just a li'l hook," Smoke said. "You walked into it."

The creamed corn had drawn blood. My lips were busted, a gash split my forehead.

"That's enough," he said. "I'm too big for you."

I got up, kicked the creamed corn aside, went after him. Science had taken a powder. I went after him, swinging stupidly, like a drunk trying to catch a butterfly.

He held me back with a gentle jab or two, then clinched me close and said, "That'll do, Cassius."

Upstairs, Mom looked at the blood on me, then said to Smoke, "Well?"

"He's okay," Smoke said with a shrug. "Plenty of desire, anyhow."

This bout proved I wasn't Young Griffo, but Jack was yet so far ahead of me I felt compelled to at last get off the dime and do *something*. I decided I should become either a famous hippie or a war hero. The different myths dueled in my fantasies: Iwo Jima, Woodstock, knapsacks, bayonets, body paint, love-ins, night patrols, Chesty Puller, Henry David Thoreau, The Jefferson Airplane, and The Shores of Tripoli.

Two months later I figured hippies were too topical, and joined the Marines.

As the shadows stretched full-length, we loaded the black bags onto the truck. We worked easily together, at a slow pace, as befits the newly rich. The stumps of the Razorback Red stalks blended into the landscape of less valuable plants nicely, reassuringly. Once we'd cashed this crop in you'd have to know just where to look to find the grow site.

Now and again we'd pause to gloat over especially well-formed buds, feeling a heady mix of fresh avarice and green-thumb pride.

During one rest, after a splash of iced tea, Smoke said, "I'm hoping to buy my way out of that Kansas warrant, see."

"You think?"

"My lawyer thinks. I have to catch up my payments to him, first, don't you know. But he figures ten grand might get the facts remembered different, and charges dropped."

"If it doesn't?"

"Shit," Smoke said. "I can keep on hidin' down here, only with better beer and better scotch." He gave me a shove, and grinned so that the scar on his forehead wriggled. "And you, baby bro?"

"I don't know," I said. "Head back west, maybe. Write another book."

"You need a hit, don't you."

"I need a hook. It takes a hook to get a hit. A publicity hook, I mean."

"I don't want no part of that," Smoke said. "Publicity."

"Yeah, but I need it."

"You only just think you need it."

About two heartbeats shy of dark we finished the grunt work. The bags were stacked into the truck bed, open ends toward the cab. We were wiping our bodies free of debris, leaves and gnats and so on that had gloomed to our sweat, when I went still, thinking I'd heard a bad sound.

"Something wrong?" Smoke asked.

"Maybe not."

I led us toward the sound, a muted mechanical growling. Smoke chambered a round in the shotgun, and I had the ladystinger in hand. We gentled toward the dry bed of Gum Creek, taking it slow, until we saw her.

A young girl, maybe fourteen, with fabulously long hair, lustrous black hair, sat on a dirt bike across the creek bed. She wore bib overalls and boondocker boots. She made eye contact with us, I think, and I believe she smirked, or smiled a little. I think Smoke and me both thought about shooting her, right then, right there, not fucking around. She snorted and shook her head, as if she held our hesitation in contempt, then smugly popped a wheelie and blew away toward the bridge.

"Aw, shit," Smoke said as we watched.

The girl's black hair spread wide about her, as would the great wings of something eager to feed on the dead.

"I know," I said. "That girl can't be no kind of news but bad."

22

This Dream Means It

Our county was named after an early pioneer who I suspect couldn't quite spell his own name. Moses Howl put up the first trading hut hereabouts, over at the main spring, near where the picnic park in West Table is now, in 1847. I'm fairly certain ol' Moses lost a vowel off his surname along the trail between the Carolinas and the Ozarks, but the short version has been cemented into history, and ours is a misspelled county on Missouri maps to this day. I don't know that anyone hung a name on West Table but nature. Our town is on a flat, a plains, a table, west of the river, between distant hills, and the name likely came about through common usage, just as a fat boy becomes Pudge or a bully becomes Buster.

I drove the Volvo carrying Niagra and Damned Spot to Pritchard's on the square. The tires barked when I steered off the rock road and onto the slab roads of town. We passed the sign, the civic booster sign that says IF YOU LIVED HERE YOU'D BE HOME NOW.

"I loved the way it looked," Niagra said.

"What's that?"

"All them money plants hung upside down to dry in the barn. The smell, the way it looked, I loved all that."

"It is encouraging," I said. "Uplifting."

There are some fine houses to gawk at when passing through West Table. Victorian mansions built by the high-gloss goobers of the town back when Victorian was a fresh style. These notable places still tend to be referred to by the surnames of the families that built them, though said families seldom own them yet. The concept of zoning never caught on here, too undemocratic to knuckle to, I suppose, so in between mansions and merely nice homes there are plenty of dumps, shacks. A perfectly maintained Victorian with a spruced lawn will have for a neighbor a shotgun shanty with a screen door that's sprung and a porch that teeters and bare dirt for a yard. This is the sort of cranky democracy hill folk insist upon, but it's also the sort of squatters' pluralism that tends to stunt what the real estate types term "appreciation." This aspect holds West Table back from ever becoming broadly picturesque, though it can be so in squinty portions.

Damned Spot rode on the backseat and had the window down, doing that dog thing, muzzle pointed into the breeze, that apparently gives mutts this weird big kick I've never quite figured out. Her paws had muddied up Lizbeth's fine upholstery some, and Damned Spot also clawed at the cloth now and again to maintain balance, which I appreciated.

We parked just off the square, to the side of Pritchard's.

They sell groceries there, and dry goods, and rent out videos. The store was cooled to nearly cold, and me and Niagra lounged in the ice-cream section awhile, the climate providing such relief.

I grabbed a cart and led over to the soda pop aisle. Our selection was easy—Coke. Those big plastic jugs. One Coke, two Coke, six Coke, a dozen.

Niagra got a half-gallon of vanilla ice cream, and we added that to the dozen jugs of Coke. The cart looked like maybe we were fixin' to go home and try'n catch diabetes.

But we were on a mission, as Smoke believed Co-Cola worked best for squaring up the pounds. A li'l warm Coke splashed on the dope helped the greenery clot good and make pretty bricks.

The checker was one of those old gals who has switched her do color away from the naturally occurring shades of head hair, toward a sort of blue that aged femmes must think makes their pink cheeks look fresher in contrast. Or something.

She rang us up, counting out the jugs. It was harvest time in the hills, and those old gals aren't stupid. She just smiled, though, and stole a look or two at me. I'd known her once, before that hair went blue.

Finally she says, "Do I know you, hon?"

"Yes, Mrs. Pritchard."

She paused to stare, then asked the most direct and crucial of down-home questions. "Who're your people?"

"Redmonds."

"My word—you must be one of General Jo's, I reckon, 'cause Bill, they don't let him have kids in the pen, there, do they?"

"No," I said, and laughed. "I'm one of General Jo's."

147

"Good people," she said. "Redmonds have traded here since Daddy opened for business in thirty-three."

"I know that," I said.

"Redmonds, that was a good ol' family around here. You owe me twenty-two thirty-two, hon."

"There you go," I said, and gave her the cash. "We'll just wheel the cart to the car."

"Sure thing, hon."

I'd shoved the cart nearly to the door, and then I heard Mrs. Pritchard call to the ol' boys who hung around the cool benches at the front of the store, "That fella there's son to General Jo Redmond—remember him?"

A duo of old boys grinned and nodded, and one of them said, "Your daddy still fightin' the bottle, or has he flat surrendered to it?"

"Well," I said, "that fight never has been much of a fight."

"No. No, sir, it ain't never been."

There's no place else like home, I hope, for memories.

On the streets, as I loaded the car, I heard that bike, looked to the alley, saw those black wings flying wide and away.

Damned Spot howled.

Imaru shivered.

After lunch Big Annie stalked me. I could feel her eyes on me. Whenever I looked up, she looked away, but she didn't *go* away.

Niagra said something about me and she going to Twin Forks River, and I nodded.

Niagra wandered into the house to get ready, and that's when Big Annie decided to pounce. I was sitting with

Smoke in the shady corner of the deck, reading the *West Table Scroll,* and she came over and took a stand about a foot from my face. She had her hands on her hips, legs spread, the total wet hen stance.

She said, "She's in love with you."

"We're just goin' canoeing."

"You're her first."

"Smoke, can you drop the Volvo at Blaney Bridge for me?"

"Sure. No sweat."

"Listen to me—she's in love with you, and you're her first."

"Leave the keys on the front right."

She slapped the *Scroll* from my hands, grabbed my ponytail, and gave a hard jerk that made my eyes water.

"Big Annie!" I said.

"Now, now, Doyle," she said in a softer tone. She sat on my lap, then, and stroked my cheeks. "You're her first big love, that's all. She wants to drop mescaline and do the river with you. I've fronted her the mescaline from my hidey stash, 'cause she's growed up and tumbled *so* in love with you, but, kiddo, what I want is—Christ, the first can have a lot to do with all of them, you understand?"

She kept stroking my cheeks.

Smoke merely aped a preoccupied paterfamilias, rigorously studying his fingernails, lost in a big think. He didn't contribute so much as a harumph.

Damned Spot tried to join Big Annie on my lap but got shoved down for it.

"I only just want you to go and show my baby some fun, some *big* fun she can hold to her heart for *forever.*"

"Big Annie, that's a lot of pressure."

There went that motherly hand to my ponytail again, the hard jerk, the tears.

"You can damned sure be extra nice to her at least, can't you?"

"Hell, yes."

"*Memorably* nice."

"I can do that."

She hadn't let go of my ponytail yet, and she said, "I know you *will,* too. Don't I?"

So, we took a slow, mescaline-enhanced float on a clean, clear stream, scuttling over orange rocks in the shallow riffles, spinning languorously out of control at the larger pools. The high bluffs gave good shadow even in the heat of the day. The water ran cold from the many springs that fed into it, the bottom fist-sized stones and long gray slab rocks that were always visible at any depth. Fish were frequently on view, as if suspended on display to be studied and admired, or lunged at with open hands and no chance at all. Trout, sucker, panfish, and silver shiners passed in the shadow of the canoe.

It was purt near to rapture, really, floating on mescaline and spring water, in a rubber canoe, with a beautiful girl, slapping a paddle into the stream now and again to fully participate. There was beer, and Luckies, and a couple of sticks of weed whose effect was redundant and puny, what with that mescaline running free through our blood and brains.

Niagra lay in my arms, a dope-grin on her face almost constantly. When we'd slide beneath limbs that held sunning snakes, hog snakes and cottonmouths and such, she cuddled up so sweetly and lowered her face to my chest. We kissed a bunch, tongue wrestled and so on.

Somewhere along The Twin Forks, the drugs took over the spare rooms in our brains, and things got a trifle tottery, hard to follow. Especially words.

"Is this a episode?" Niagra asked.

"Huh?"

"Am I a episode to you?"

"I'm not, you know, *having* an episode—am I?"

"To be only a episode—that would sell our love cheap."

"Episode? I'm not there."

When other canoes passed us, and the occupants shouted howdy, all we could muster were smiles in return. We seldom looked where we were going, hardly steered, just took our river journey one leap of faith at a time. Niagra's pretty hand rested on my stomach, and my stomach, see, ain't really that far from my testicles. She'd rub my belly and my dick would tingle. That is, of course, the fun angle to sex and drugs, that the senses run off the chain and the mind just eggs them on toward foolish splendors. A little breath in your ear, or a foot rub, can feel like six with-it lovers are hummin' your tune in concert.

Mind dope has always made me horny. A horny liquid of high-proof want. Once, on Guam, after I'd been busted from lance corporal back to private, I worked the main gate, wearing my official tropical pith helmet and a red lanyard and white web belt with a forty-five strapped to my side, tripping on something called Orange Speckle Acid. I got intensely into my assigned task of waving vehicles through the gate, lost my soul to the job, snapping salutes that trailed sparks at all and sundry, even those passers not of the salute-required class. I was a magic Marine until two women, Aussie tourists I believe, asked me where some-place was and I apparently just walked off, deserted my post, and began to follow their slim, tanned legs. I was in a dreamscape of carnal want, and thought those tanned legs and attached felt likewise. I have this recollection of being several hundred yards off post, and the Aussie gals were going on about how I can't come with them. Go home, they were saying, like you would to a super dumb dog. The sergeant of the guard, an almost college graduate named Liggett, took me away from them, laughing hard, and said, "I told you not to drop a whole tab."

I finished my duty, slathering immense, fiery style onto my movements, Sergeant Liggett watching closely over me. When my shift was up, he said, "Today, Redmond, you were the best goddamn Marine I've ever seen you be." On the ride back to the barracks he pulled the duty truck off the main road, onto a jungle rut, which I thought might just be the animal path to the center of the earth, and gave me a blow job I still think I remember. I don't go for men that way, before nor since, but it was like a movie edited all wrong that I had no conscious part in. When I came I blossomed into a star, something brilliant in the jet stream.

I've had a slew of blow jobs since then, all from females, some on drugs, but, *lordy,* truth to tell, there was never none of them better at pure-dee cocksuckin' than that ol' sergeant of the guard.

"I feel funny," Niagra said. "But good."

The sun had gotten caught up in her hair, and she looked ready to burst into beams. On we floated. A thought hit me, and I chased after it until I could say it.

"You know," I said, "when it comes to outlaws, the

ones I most admire are the ones whose names you never hear. Really, that's the kind to be."

"I hear frogs. It's too early for frogs. What's that I hear?"

"I said something—could that be it?"

Cave mouths are abundant in the bluffs above the river, caves stocked with thumb bats and lizard bones, and the river decided which we should stop at. The current jammed the canoe onto a gravel bank, next to a slender path, and up the path yawned a cave.

We got out, knowing what would happen somewhere along that path or in that cave.

"I love you," Niagra said. "And this river."

"You, too," I said.

Not far up the path she stopped. I was already yanking at her halter straps. She said, "You'n me, Doyle, we will do shit that lives on for forever. That's my dream, and I mean it."

Niagra gargled beer at the river's edge, and I had my hands in the water, swishing and rubbing them.

I said, "I better wash that one finger mighty good."

She gave me a look, a sidelong happy look, then spit foamy beer into the stream.

"Some of those things we just done, Doyle—I never knew normal men liked *that*."

"I can't speak for normal men—but *I* liked it, every bit."

"Mm-hmm. You did."

"You didn't seem to hate a bit of it yourself, darlin'."

"I've got no claim on normal, neither. Praise the Lord."

* * *

153

About supper time we hit Blaney Bridge. I could see the Volvo parked in a clear spot beside the road.

We weren't at all straight, yet, but the sunshine and elements had worn us down. The canoe deflated in a few minutes, we packed it into the trunk, and split.

There is this karmic force loose in my life that dictates that if I've, say, dropped mescaline and smoked weed and drunk beer and spent the afternoon along a riverbank fuckin' 'til my toes curl back, I will be stopped by the law before I get home.

Sheriff Lilley pulled me over, lights flashing, on BB Highway, not ten minutes from Big Annie's. I got out, stood by the driver's door, and he whipped up and got in my face.

"I've had phone calls, Redmond," he said. "From far off in Californey."

"They can do anything these days, all the wires and poles and shit."

His eyes hid behind mirrored shades. He grinned. That big mustache of his twitched as his lips moved.

"You know we're related?"

"Yeah," I said, "I know that."

"That's the only reason I didn't just now bust you in your smart mouth and whip your ass all over this road in front of your girlfriend, there." He shoved me, fingertips to my chest. "Your wife out yonder says this car is stolen, son. She's been on the long-distance, fixin' to get your butt tossed in jail."

"That sounds like her."

Sheriff Lilley bent down and looked at Niagra.

"Girl, you know this car was stolen?"

Niagra, bless her young heart, said, "No, sir. Not to my acknowledgment."

"You know now," he said. He seemed to relax some; in fact, he made a noise I can only call a chortle. "Listen, son, I've had breakups, I understand how ridiculous and mean these deals can get. Just send this car on back to the screamin' lady. She holds the legal title."

"Uh-huh," I said. "So her new boyfriend can drive it." That hit him where he lived.

"Oh, now I see. It's that way, is it? She didn't quite tell me that."

I wanted a Lucky in the worst way. I got one to my lips, but the lighter, soaked, I guess, just gave off sparks and wouldn't flame. The sideshow of sparks appealed to the mescaline yet in me, I think, because I really became obsessed with making that fucker light. After what may well have been a hundred or so fruitless flicks, Sheriff Lilley said, "Jesus Christ, son, you want some fire for that son of a bitch or you just aimin' to make me crazy with that *flick, flick, flick* shit?"

"Fire," I said.

He pulled out a burnished Zippo with a lariat etched into it, gave me a light.

"Damn," he said. "Hope that cigarette tastes like heaven, son, you worked hard enough for it."

"I guess I'm determined."

"You're somethin', all right," he said. "Somethin' I could probly hang thirty days on you for, right here and now. But, hell, I ain't in the mood." He actually patted my shoulder, gave a squeeze, politicking me. Sheriffs have to get elected by such as I. "That car will go on hot sheets

155

pretty soon. Now, I'm not gonna put it on tomorrow, 'cause these marital things are so chickenshit and all. I been *there,* my own self. But, hell, in about three days I'll have to put out an alert, so you've got 'til then to settle this shit with your wife."

" 'Preciate it," I said. "We're cousins, right?"

"Just butthole cousins," he said. He walked toward his car. "And don't put too much stock in what that amounts to. You've got yourself three days, then you'll see me again. You won't be happy to see me."

He left the lights whirling as he pulled away, and I just watched and watched, thinking, Imaru, Imaru, is this still research? Or am I livin' it now?

23

Incas Drink Free

Juke joint, roadhouse, honky-tonk, barrelhouse, nitespot, Devil's Spigot, bucket of blood, and Serengeti watering hole—all are terms that applied to The Inca Club. It's a barn-sized venue built of wooden ties, in an octagonal shape, with the look of a readily defensible frontier fort. There's no sign out front, but there is a wide, chalk-dust parking lot and plenty of activity. The Inca Club has been spilling drunks onto Highway 160 since Highway 160 was merely Overlook Road, back about 1944.

Warriors returning from the Big One ached for a place to sit around in and get drunk hidden from civilian eyes, so Tom Wofford put a place up for them and named it The Inca Club, after a set of warriors who'd entirely disappeared. They say he lost money until the legendary shindig of July Fourth, 1947, after which he finally started charging veterans for each and every drink. Before then patriotism and sadness had combined to make him by far the most generous barkeep a Dogface, Squid, or Jarhead had ever known.

Big Annie knew a customer for our product named David Anglin, who I sort of knew, too, from research hours spent at The Inca Club when I'd hung about town "visiting" Panda, visits which ranged from a week or so to, if I was broke or Lizbeth was feeling inspired by my grittily evocative homeland and between teaching gigs, three or four months. Anglin was a pretty good ol' boy, a former deputy who'd switched sides and sold a lot of weed up around St. Louis, and Carbondale, Illinois. He operated a crossroads market down Double-K Highway that didn't seem nearly prosperous enough to afford his big house, bass and pontoon boats, young pretty wife dressed in Nudie's of Nashville attire, or vacations to Marco Island.

"Anglin thinks he wants the whole crop," Big Annie said. "But he'll need to give it a taste first, naturally."

I went to The Inca looking for Anglin, and I went alone. The gang felt jumpy, so the others were on gun patrol around the barn, the bricks of crop, our futures.

The Inca Club was, of course, a bit dark inside, the way drunks and rogue flirts want it to be. Mr. Wofford sat at the end of the bar watching his workers barely work. He wore fancy bib overalls, black with silver studs along the seams, and a starched short-sleeve white shirt. His face was dominated by shades with sort of red lenses, the kind optometrists make some folk wear, though he may have worn them purely for style.

He waved at me, said, "Hey, Dukie boy!" which is his usual greeting to everyone.

He was acquainted with me and all of mine. I know he knew me, though my front name might slip him.

I ordered beer in a bottle. There was a sign on the wall behind the bar that read INCAS DRINK FREE. There's a bold promise that wouldn't ever cost Mr. Wofford any bottles of brew. Not unless Imaru checked in with a new report, anyhow.

Anglin was there, toward the back, sitting on the fender of a red '57 Chevy shell. Mr. Wofford had added the classic Chevy to the decor so customers could sit on the backseat, snuggle, and imbibe as they had when frisky and young, but it led to so many broken-bottle scraps over time allotments that he'd finally yanked the seats, but left the shell.

"Hey, Doyle," Anglin said. "That is you, ain't it?"

"Every damn day," I said. "How you been?"

"Been gettin' ham fat and dollar strong." Anglin was probably forty-seven, forty-eight, and pretty proud of himself. He looked like a surly dumpling. As to size, he'd be a hard middleweight if he shed seventy pounds of soft suet. Only maybe five eight, but somehow haulin' two hundred and thirty or forty pounds around. One of those. He dressed kind of uptown for our region: snakeskin boots, silky black shirt, string tie, custom cowpoke chapeau—all that ritzy Americana shit. "Big Annie run you over?"

"She didn't come with."

"Oh." His career called for paranoia, and he sort of flinched. "Now I know her *good*," he said, "but I never did know you this way, Doyle. No offense."

"You know my name, though. You know my people."

That stalled him. He took some deep breaths that set his fat loose so it shimmied. He tipped his hat.

"Damned right," he said. "Pardon fuckin' me, won't you?"

It was about four in the afternoon, and the jukebox exclusively played shitkicker moans, loud. Workaday Jacks and Jills were getting early starts on their pay-night toots, and several construction workers and such were thanking God it's Friday. The noise forced conversations to be practically pantomimed, so many comments requiring clarification that were best made by hand gestures and silent mouthings.

But I got Anglin's point, and he got mine.

He walked me to the parking lot, and we shook hands, hee-hawed at an unfunny joke, slapped backs, enacting the whole cornpone skit of outlaw camaraderie. During his biggest smile I noted that his teeth were of the picture-perfect and false kind.

In the Volvo, driving away, my head just rang and rang with music, over and over, but the tune was never anything but "Peace in the Valley."

Funny, huh?

24

The Point of the Country

So, the next afternoon was a shady afternoon spent in Big Annie's kitchen. The ladies were trimming buds with pinking shears, and Smoke and me used a trash compactor and liberal doses of Co-Cola to square up bricks of Razorback Red. Truthfully, we only halfway knew what we were doing. You wouldn't call us serious dope growers, or outlaws shrewd about commerce. Our scales were big spenders, extra generous, I think. Some of those two-pound bricks seemed a lot closer to three.

The stereo accompanied us all day long with Johnny Cash and Steve Young and Koko Taylor and the Stray Cats, some Doors, Little Milton, Willie Nelson, and Santana, plus Niagra's favorite, Marilyn Monroe sings Golden Hits. We drank pop that wouldn't be required for the bricks, inhaled our fresh product, felt oh so happy and verging on rich, dreams alive and almost in hand.

Could life be better?

The phone blatted. Niagra answered it, said "Huh?" a few times, each "Huh?" a testimonial to the quality of our gardening results, then handed the receiver off to Smoke. He stood by the fridge, said, "Hey, how're you?" and, "Yeah, okay. Sure."

He hung up, grinned a li'l sickly grin.

"The folks are in town."

"Uh-huh," I said.

"They want a pow-wow, lickety-split, over at Panda's."

"Whatta you think, big bro?"

"Aw, shit—I owe it to 'em, I guess. They've stood up pretty good, all this time." He shook his dreadlocks loose, took a big long suck on a joint the size of a carrot. "It's just, I *know* what they'll have to say."

"Oh, you bet," I said. "I can hear it all twice, here and now."

Mom's a stalwart sweetheart and slow to anger. She stands near five ten, a giant, practically, amongst her own generation, and has come to weigh near one eighty, beef to the heels, honestly, but affects a coquettish manner. She colors her hair chestnut, smiles to acknowledge or avoid, and flushes pink when she tells dirty jokes. Men who aren't scared by her healthy stature have always flocked about her, responding to her macabre "I'm just a frail li'l blossom in a mighty high breeze" act, a scene I'd often witnessed, if never totally comprehended its success.

She spread a dinner for the pack of us as the hot edge faded from the afternoon. Fried baloney sandwiches with thick tomato slices, slathered in mayo. A plain meal that makes its point, and one of my favorites. It's a sandwich that in therapy I learned was among my "comfort foods"—deep knowledge that failed to ruin it for me.

When I was younger and hard-hearted, with hot, hostile artistic ambitions I yearned to charge at the aloof, faceless "thems" of our world until they said Uncle, I believed the scariest words ever spoken to be "The apple never falls far from the tree." That whole concept inspired clinging fears in the wee hours, and a halting miserable shyness in the presence of those who seemed to be the anointed. If I fell not far from the tree, was I then fated to be, not, say, a college prof of English, but inmate 2679785? A parolee who spends seventeen years on the night shift with Custodial Services at KU Med Center in K.C., instead of a Prize-Winning Novelist with a saltbox on the Cape? An unwholesome artsy freak, and not an esteemed citizen whose voting privileges have never been revoked?

I went through those pitiful, hangdog years being ashamed of my roots and origins, referring to home as "our place in the country," and to my father as a "self-made man." I hung my head and eenie-meenie-minie-moed when confronted at dinner tables by too many forks. I tried to give the impression that slapping an uppity snotnose silly was not the sort of act contained in my portfolio.

It must surely have been noticeable and insufferable to my folks, so obvious were my feelings, until, I don't know why, the shame passed. My attitude shifted, the twang twanged once more into my speaking voice. Maybe it was all the Faulkner, or Algren, or Whitman. Anyway, I quickly came back down to the raising I had gotten above, and let every nuance of my sartorial style and social preferences and personal anecdotes cop to it right up front—I yam what I yam, and beg your pardon, sir, but go fuck yourself if you don't like it.

On this evening, there Panda sat, as ever at the head of the table, battered and imperial, and I couldn't watch Mom's big hands halving those sandwiches without wondering: When their eyes met, were those goo-goo eyes?

A bottle each of Johnnie Red and Cutty Sark sat on the table, glass tributes to a petty argument General Jo and Panda have kept going for a decade or more; to wit, which is better?

I drank some of each, conflicted loyalties at work on me, ate a sandwich, and said, "This is just wonderful."

"Ain't it just?" Mom said.

"I love it when we're flocked this way," General Jo said. "A family." He showed his opinion of the Cutty by keeping it flowing, each new pour registering on Panda's face like yet another pointed insult to his overall taste and scotch whisky expertise. General Jo is more my height than Smoke's, though he weighs twenty pounds less. He's got a lovely head of gray curly hair that many a toupeed millionaire might like to bid on or steal. There's a dipshit jail tattoo of a Confederate flag on his right forearm, but the whole thing is in a faded blue color and not worth a damn. When he smiles, these very appealing dimples appear in his cheeks, and he smiles a lot for a career janitor whose done such hard time in Jeff City and Korea and, I imagine, his very own head.

I feel I'm his sequel. I feel I inherited my storytelling instincts from him, though I've somewhat refined them. General Jo tends to be snockered when he starts a story, and he'll get to telling one, a memory of some interest, a local tragedy, say, and you'll be listening tight, then he'll get thoroughly bogged down in the inconsequential details, such as just what *was* the name of the fourth fella on the porch when the runaway timber truck hit the house, and pretty soon you're not listening tight anymore, or even at all, until finally a silence butts in and you or I say, "Well, General Jo, the name don't matter—it's the truck that counts."

General Jo reached across the table, poured a triple slug of Cutty into my glass, and smiled a great one.

"How's my boy?" he asked.

Man, did Imaru hear that!

No argument could sway Smoke. He dismissed them all as being so puny the hens wouldn't peck them.

"When I get this money I'm fixin' to get, I'll come up and set things right with the tired-ass law."

"And this'll be when?" Mom asked.

"Not long."

"And the money, I mean, darlin', I don't aim to *pry,* but where's it comin' from?"

"This'n that."

"I see." She smiled and fanned her face with a copy of the *Scroll,* her big forearms flexin' like gator tails. Panda sat in the other room to watch the Cardinals, so it was just our li'l nuclear unit locked in debate. "Wouldn't be anything *criminal,* would it?"

"Not very, really," Smoke said. He flapped a hand at me, an appeal for support.

"It depends who you ask," I said. "There's various philosophies afield."

Boy howdy, did General Jo start to perk up at the

mention of crime! The ol' hound, God bless him, heard the bugle, smelled that smell. He popped up from the rocker he'd been in silently for ten minutes or so, drink in hand, and began to pace. The fingers on his free hand started to rub together, over and over. It was touching, and I couldn't have loved him more. There was an appetite in him that hadn't been satisfied, I don't guess, since he made parole and squared up so long ago. When I'd passed through K.C. in Lizbeth's Volvo, and we'd worked together, spray painting it, and ripping off local plates outside a pizza joint, he'd beamed and worked with an air of unleashed pleasure.

The wall of dead, he needed their nods, too, as much as all of us.

"What sort of crime is it?" he asked.

"There's various philosophies afield," I said.

"Plain spoken," he said. "In English."

"Dope," Smoke said. "Smokin' dope."

"Ah," General Jo responded, and you could see his hopes deflating. I mean, he was an armed robber by nature, see, not the breed of miscreant who sneaks around, growing shit in the woods and peddlin' it by the Baggie. *"Farmers."*

"There's money in it," Smoke said. He walked over to General Jo and slapped a bear hug on him, raised him aloft, a sign of affection that has always made our dad, the ex-convict, giggle and wiggle and turn red in the face. When Smoke set him down, he said, "I was plannin' to gift you two or three bricks, there, General Jo, but if it's too chickenshitted for you, then the hell with it."

"What weight to the brick?" Mom asked. "And what do the kids pay for it these days?"

GIVE US A KISS

"A couple of pounds to the brick," I said. "General Jo, all those janitors you know, you could, maybe . . ."

He waggled his head, then nodded.

"But I'm a juicer."

"He don't know the prices," Mom said. "We'd need to know the prices of the different assortments, sizes, whatnot."

"Sell it for two hundred per fat ounce," Smoke said, "and your janitor crew'll think you're Santa Claus."

So there we were, in the ancestral parlor, the eyes from the wall of dead taking us in, watching, making Imaru feel eternal, every dead head on our tree itching to nod.

Mom's and General Jo's eyes met. I could practically hear their brain cells crunching the numbers, until Mom said, "Sixteen, ain't it? Ounces to the pound?"

"Times two hundred," Smoke said.

The folks acted cool until the numbers tallied. The promising math totals caused Mom to smile and begin to flush, and General Jo held his arms spread and said, "Give us a kiss." Then they gave it up, guffawed and hugged and kissed each other, their old feet dancing, bodies whirling, making our house rock, and I looked at the hanging pictures, and, oh, yeah, I saw what I looked for.

25

Tuffy Just Bristles Up at That Color Moon

There was a reddish rut, carved into the earth in sinuous curls and dips and pinched curves, leading up to Anglin's cabin. We'd had to shove open a metal gate suspended between oak-stump posts when we turned from where the red rut met the rock road. The cabin sat on the backside of Anglin's three hundred acres, across a ridge from his main house, and on a different road altogether.

I rode in the truck bed, lollygagging atop our stack of harvested bricks. The bricks were all wrapped in black plastic, and they felt good in my hands, substantial and potent, and were pretty to look at. The smell of dope, that scent of exotic hay, a magical barn aroma, rose from the bricks and lay heavy and sweet on the wind.

Niagra drove, slow-footed on the clutch but safely, while Big Annie occupied Smoke's lap. She sat with her back to the passenger window, one arm extended around the cab, and she made several attempts to yank my ponytail. I could detect the fumes of scotch exhalations from both the cab and my own mouth. The gang of us had our hopes up high. Smoke and Big Annie had smooched and giggled since about Gum Creek, and funny things were apparently being said outside my earshot since so much laughter leaked from the cab and rippled back to me.

The cabin came into view when we topped a swale, a li'l hillock bald of trees but thick with tall horseweed and the like.

I smacked a hand against the rear glass of the cab.

"Hold it a sec," I said as Niagra slowed. "Let's scope it out some."

The truck came to a complete halt, and the headlights were doused. The gang got out, walked to the front, stood by the grill, and stared down at the cabin.

A dog barked, and you could hear a chain snapping as the hound strained. Peepers peeped, and lightning bugs were fanned out across the meadow, flickering by the dozens.

Big Annie seemed to shiver, and she crossed her arms.

"Is this in tune?" she asked.

"Tune? What tune, darlin'?" Smoke said.

"The right tune."

I imagine it was ten o'clock, give or take. The moon was low in the sky and fat, nearly full, and floated like a bobber in the sky. It had that yellow color, the hue of cheese gone bad, and the yellow light it cast seemed to tint objects as well as illuminate them. The cabin wasn't much: an old woodsman's shack, with a rough plank porch and rails made of seasoned saplings. Lanterns burned inside, throwing light out two big front windows. A stone chimney showed. Strangler vines grew up the porch and the porch rails and the chimney, too, and were inching toward the door. A new pickup truck sat near the porch steps.

The howling dog was chained to the porch rail, and I could see silhouettes of a small barn and a toolshed on down the slope beyond the cabin.

"Does this feel in tune?" Big Annie said again. Her hinky mood was infectious and encouraged flinches and second thoughts. "I'm not sure we're in tune here."

The dog was barking his throat raw, and that didn't soothe our intuitions any.

"There ain't no tune," Smoke said. "There ain't no goddamn tune at all." He slapped the fender. "Let's just go on down'n get rich."

Niagra pushed next to me, and I draped an arm over her shoulders.

She whispered, "Your big brother is almost looney, know it? I mean, you're *both* almost looney, but Smoke's more almost."

"How can you tell?" I asked, but she didn't answer.

"Hop in," she said. "Ride."

Loose in my own bones again, I hopped from the truck bed, waggling a select black brick. Anglin had come onto the plank wood porch, holding a bottle of beer, nodding. He'd missed a button on his blue, sleeveless work shirt, and his flab stretched the opening to showcase a hairy belly button.

"Golly, yes," he said. "Let's *do* have a taste."

The light cast through the cabin windows was irregular in shape but bright enough. The dog howled and whimpered and howled.

Niagra backed the truck in to the steps, then Smoke and Big Annie spilled from the cab. I made my way up the steps, but the strangler vines were in shadow and I stepped into them, boots trapped in the tangle, until I kicked my way free.

On the porch Anglin reached for the brick, took it, then leaned in close to me and said, "Shit, budso, I figured it to be only just you and your brother, there. Didn't figure you'd haul the girls along on a weed deal."

"They're full partners."

"You got that right." Anglin inhaled deeply, then released the air and expansively claimed, "That truck sure smells like money." Then, he spun to the side. "Tuffy! Tuffy! Goddamnit—hush!"

"What *is* with that dog?" Big Annie asked.

"The moon," Anglin offered. "Tuffy just bristles up at that color moon." He glanced up at the yellow moon trolling across the sky like stinky-cheese bait for bottom feeders. He stepped aside then and waved the brick toward the cabin door. "Mi casa su casa, folks. We'll twist a stick and do bizness—hey?"

In the cabin, by lanterns' glow, Big Annie bent over a barrel-top table to roll a joint. The barrel had bullet holes in the body and knife gouges on the top. Big Annie frowned some as she twisted the stick, the white skin between her brows bunching up. I observed her technique with the same variety of pleasure I might derive from close scrutiny of a manicurist or a fine mechanic. She pinched the weed out, minced it between fingertips onto a single Tops paper. The dog noises prompted her eyes to wander, but she rolled a perfect joint, then licked it into a moist and splendid symmetrical beauty.

Anglin said, "Lordy, girl, whenever'd you roll your first joint, huh?"

Big Annie gave him a wink.

"I don't recall," she said. Her tone was just a li'l bit larded with pride. "At Freedom Hall, up in K.C., whenever it was the MC5 played there. Ever hear of them? Back in those days."

Smoke crouched forward, held some fire to the joint, and Big Annie inhaled, nodding.

But—that dog! The dog seemed berserk, almost, yanking his chain and howling. Me and Niagra crossed glances, then sidled over to the open cabin doorway. It was hard to see much. Anglin had taken the smoke, had a suck, and said, "Oh, yeah, this'll fetch the price."

That's when the shadows moved down by the barn, shadows doing various styles of crouching, stooping, but moving. I saw that long hair fly out from a dark form, a silhouette of vulture wings across the dirt yard.

"Get in the truck," I told Niagra, then turned to Anglin. "Say, Dave?" Anglin's face shifted some at my surly vocal pitch. "That girl out there, with all the hair?"

"My niece, on the wife's side—what about her?"

"She needs a haircut."

The ladystinger, it just bloomed into my hand, and I took casual aim at Anglin, who just stood there, joint in his mouth, looking like he was suddenly having to hear the *exact joke* he'd wanted to tell. I shot him somewhere around the kneecap, and blood and blue jean tufts, threads, really, flew. He fell forward, hurt leg blown straight back, and thudded on his chest.

"Hey!" Big Annie shouted. "Hey, hey, hey!"

"They're out there," I told them. "Dollys."

26

Blood on Blood

Smoke and me leaked a blood trail. We'd both been punched open while sliding down from that dirt road to the gully. They'd gotten too close to us. Things happened so quickly—Dollys moving this way, that way, Tuffy the dog howling on his leash. I was still hearing Anglin's fingers break, a pop like shingles snapping, from when he'd reached for his pistol, blood gurgling from around his knee, but Smoke reached him first. Anglin said some shit about Bunk, Bunk Dolly, and did we think they were all stupid, or what? Smoke treated Anglin's fingers like celery stalks to arrange around a bowl of dip, and the man screamed in a truly memorable manner. I thought about killing him, but I thought too long, then the chance of it was gone.

Their numbers were just a guess—three, I reckon, and that damned dog. They'd sprayed us with shot up on the dirt road, birdshot or some such, certainly not buckshot or else the Redmond line would've ended, most likely, in the wet muck of that dark gully.

Smoke and me slammed ourselves into the thicket beyond the gully. We hurled our bodies into the brush and tangle of limbs and rocks. Springer and the Dolly thug puppies were on the high road, shouting and chambering rounds. Their car sat there, steam rising from the hood, at least one tire flat, and the headlight Smoke and me both missed still shining.

I hugged the ground, put my nose in the dirt. I felt that my breathing was loud, amplified by tension, and might be a giveaway, even so far up as the road. My left haunch hurt, a bevy of stings, and I ran my hand along there and came back with blood.

Springer stood on the road, the metal thing over his nose I'd busted for him shining; I saw him quite clearly, and that damned Tuffy jumped and strained at his leash, eager to track us and eat us.

I'd shot off all my bullets.

I guess I knew this was *the* night, that long grisly night my reckless soul and sensibility have been haunting me, just fucking *haunting* me, to find and live out since practically the toddler stage.

The stink-cheese moon didn't help us any to hide. Smoke had been hurt worse than me. The shotgun spray caught him all around and about his right armpit. The meat of his biceps looked ground, ready to pattie and fry. Even in the night I could see blood sliding down his arm to his fist.

Between us we'd chummed enough blood on the night wind that even I, with mere human capacity, could smell

it, and any ol' worthless dog would, too, and track us in
under a minute.

We'd come out of Anglin's cabin blasting away, as in a
legendary moment from our ancestors' lives. That girl
with the hair, the hair and the dirt bike, zoomed ahead of
us. I believe she intended to lock the gate between the oak
stumps, cage us in. But Niagra got the truck rolling along
the red rut and caught up to the girl. She goosed the truck
into the rear wheels of the dirt bike, and shoved the girl
ass-over-tea-kettle ahead of us and into a giant shrub. The
shrub caught the girl in its tangle, and the headlights made
a picture of her, meshed in the limbs, four feet above
ground, held there like a ritual offering to some potent
god or other.

On down that dirt road, a road I don't know the name
of, me and Smoke told Niagra to let us hop out. Niagra
screamed, "Did I kill her? Huh? Did I just kill someone?"
I hadn't an answer. Smoke said, "Get the truck to Panda's.
Stash it in the garage—you've got to get that load away
from here!"

The ladies split, and I'd say we slowed the Dollys, sure
enough.

Smoke scooted under the low branches, over to me.
There were blood spots misted on his cheek, around his
eyes. He leaned his face to mine, put his lips to my ear. His
beard tickled.

"How're you set, baby bro?"

"No more bullets."

"Fuck this shit, anyhow."

"I got shot in the ass."

"I ain't dying on my knees."

And then I felt my brother's hand, and I reached over

and took hold of it. We held hands that way for a minute or so. The Dollys were shouting their version of our near futures at us, which I didn't need to hear. The hand-holding offered comfort, as a last cigarette does, maybe, while the firing squad loads.

I heard Tuffy before I saw him, and when I saw him he was right on us. Up close, I'd say his heritage included a mastiff, and maybe a bluetick, something like that. He howled around our legs, jumped and snapped, and I kicked at him and he clamped onto my ankle. My scream made us a target.

I pulled my leg high, and that pulled Tuffy close, and I reached a hand under his jowls, and choked him. As my grip tightened his jaw relaxed, fell away from my ankle. The sounds he made will hang with me. I rolled him onto his back, put both hands to his throat. He beat at me with his paws, scratched me on the chest, along my chin and cheek. I put my body weight to work, dropped both knees to his belly, and squeezed my hands.

Shots were fired, and leaves gave off that sound, the one of rain in a gust. To be hunted like wild boars by dogs and Dollys in the forest where we'd been born—it seemed so right!

Tuffy's tongue lolled from the side of his mouth, his paws still pawing but with no vigor, and I heard bones pop.

I fell away.

His paws sort of jerked again, then he was still and limp.

I started to cry, just blubber and bubble.

"I'm a damned *dog* killer, now!"

"Shh."

My ankle felt like, like—a dog had bit it.

Smoke set off up the hill, one arm flopping, the other dangling the shotgun, moving slow and hesitantly but keeping his profile below the ridgeline. I copied him in route and style. The muscles in my hurt ass seemed to waffle, spasm, I guess, when I strained over logs or rocks or ruts.

We could hear the Dollys, on this side of the gully now, beating noisily in the woods like they were on safari, trying to flush beasts both stupid and wounded.

Big bro led up the slope and to the flank, away from the sounds of our hunters. Summer weeds broke beneath our feet, and green smells and bugs filled the air. We came to a clear-cut, an open zone, and that moonlight, in that bad-cheese shade, gave our skin and blood and faces the tint of olden pictures.

"Hush your cryin'," Smoke whispered.

His tone was harsh.

I went to his side, ripped his shirt from him. His arm was all open and like a glob. I twisted the shirt around the bad section and knotted it.

"That dog, that got to me," I said.

Over the ridge, maybe two miles distant, we could see the glow of town rising to the sky.

"Let's split," he said. "I'll cut toward town, you head toward Big Annie's. We need wheels, Doyle. You get yours, find me at Panda's."

I had no chance to respond, really. We hugged, and off he went, into the thick woods. I watched my brother's back until it disappeared.

I stood there a moment, my ass hurtin' and all these crazy comments filled my head. Stuff for Imaru, I guess.

Then I lit out, guessing for direction, but I made good time.

Not long after we split, the night cracked with gunfire, back behind me, and the sounds circled in the hills so I couldn't be sure where they came from, though I *was* sure what they likely meant.

Uncontrollable blubbers and bubbles.

27

Call the Tune

They all raised their voices at me: Imaru this! Imaru that! Imaru will! Imaru must!

Or, could be, it was just nerves, panic, the bedlam of sudden sorrow.

I hit Gum Creek kind of fast and the Volvo bounced angrily. I kept the headlights on, but seeing the rocks didn't smooth them any. I feared ambush on the main road. The Volvo jostled and shimmied and rose and fell across the dry white roughness of the creek bed. My head thumped the roof, my butt felt the pain.

I drove on beyond the money garden a piece, kept on until Gum Creek was about to become the Howl River. I steered up the bank, but it was too steep, and I ruined a headlight against a willow sapling. I backed up and got a better run at the bank and churned the tires and booted the gas pedal and, finally, basically grated the Volvo through the dirt and debris. That cost me the muffler, but I crested onto clear ground, the back lawn of Tararum.

The car had acquired a tilt, and an angle. It didn't go exactly where aimed anymore, but still traveled more or less toward the target, only by a challenging sort of oblique flank trajectory.

At the cupola I noted the narrow walkway that wended elegantly between the trees and back up to the big house, the drumstick palace. I was on my own ground, I guess, according to those laws more ancient than law books. The Volvo fit on the path.

The unmuffled engine and the one walleyed headlight announced my presence, and as I neared Tararum I saw that eight or ten esteemed citizens in leisure togs had gathered to observe. It was midnight on Saturday, and some networking amongst the finer element was going on. I made an effort to not bust any statues, even in my grief. I skirted the swimming pool and clipped a table, just a li'l ol' patio table, and sent several glassy objects crashing. My speed was down to a prudent level.

Sam T. Byrum himself stepped in front of the car and I hit the brake. Byrum was a fairly large, regal dude. He dressed spiffy and carried himself like a natural-born champ. The kind of man I always consider whipping, but seldom get a fair chance at.

"What in the motherfucking hell do you think you're doin'?"

I leaned my head out the window. Several of Byrum's guests were saying things along the lines of idiot, white-trash fool, the usual salutations. The car roared too loudly for me to hear all.

"Well, ain't this Morningside Drive?"

"Morningside—you drunk son of a bitch."

"Oh, shit, now, hoss," I said, and pointed toward a big-ass tier of fancily trimmed and styled shrubs. "Must be that there's it."

I cut the wheel and punched the gas. The shrubs weren't that stout. They fainted at the first push and folded under the Volvo like an upstairs maid to a randy Rockefeller.

I carry a bunch of anger with me. Who I carry it for rotates.

A couple of long-stemmed glasses bounded off the rear window.

I departed via the main gate, the car steering badly, moving sort of bug-fashion. Vapors wisped from the hood.

I was born for this.

Again, I mean.

The vapors had become a cloud by the time I pulled into Panda's front yard. I crossed the yard to the door and spooked a cat, I think, and it scampered toward the graveyard. The shades were drawn, but the lights were on. A burned smell from the Volvo trailed me, and I could hear a radio playing from someone's screened porch.

I let myself in, and they were all in the living room. Big Annie and Niagra sat on the arms of the couch, too pent-up to relax. The TV set blared *Saturday Night Live,* Steve Martin hosting, I think. Panda had a cigar in hand. His blackthorn cane rested between his knees. On the coffee table there was a platter, and on it were saltine crackers and pickled pigs' feet. Only one of the pig's feet had been eaten. The others lay there, pale and glistening in their own jelly. They caught my eye. I had to stare at them for a few seconds.

"Maybe you'll tell me," Panda said to me. "What the hell is goin' on? These gals are vague. Mighty vague."

"It ain't good," I said.

I shook my head, hard, and looked away from those pigs' feet, that jelly stuff.

"I need an answer, boy. I been polite for over an hour. I laid out a spread of snacks, there, and I've been hospitable and patient—but no more."

"Your face," Niagra said. "Doyle—you're all clawed to hell!"

She hustled to me, we hugged. I guess her hand slipped below the belt. She felt blood. She turned and held her bloody hand toward her mother, her mouth open in alarm.

"I caught a shot," I said.

Big Annie's face wrecked. The features mangled.

She said, "Oh, no, oh, no, oh, no—Smoke?"

Big bro's name, raised in this fashion, brought Panda to his feet. He leaned on his cane and got in my face. His eyes, those blue, mean and dauntless fucking eyes, were all over me. I tried not looking into them, I tried scanning the photos on the wall, I tried to see, really see, the floral patterns in the faded wallpaper.

No use.

Our eyes met, and I couldn't handle the potency. Even as we stared at each other I began to cry. The muscles in my hurt ass spasmed, and I just went to bawling. I let myself fall to the floor.

Big Annie shrieked, then Niagra chimed in.

Panda didn't say a thing, not until he whacked me with

that blackthorn cane. He caught me flush across the shoulders.

"Not my baby," he said. "No, no—uh-uh."

He whacked me again.

"You measly bookworm pansy—you let them kill my boy?"

The expression on his face was way out there, out there where I'd never seen him before.

"Why"—whack—"not"—whack—"you? Why not you, not Smoke? Uh-uh. Nooo. *You!*"

I moved away, crossed the floor like a worm. The pain from the cane stunned my shoulders; my arms wouldn't move right for a li'l bit.

"I'll do what's called for!" I shouted. I was still bawling. "I know what's called for. I loved him, too, you know."

"That don't even matter!"

The ladies had stalled in their shrieking, mesmerized by my grandfather whacking the shit out of me. They had their arms flung all about each other, tears running from eyelash to chin point. Their cheeks trembled.

Panda put that cane to use for walking and left the room. I knew where he was headed. I heard the door squeak open, the one to the gun closet under the stairs. The ancient armaments would be coming out.

The ladies helped me to my feet, and we did a pitiful group hug. It felt like a hindrance, this sympathy and empathy. My course had been charted.

I broke the circle.

"Get the load to where it's safe," I said.

Big Annie looked at me and shook her head.

"Man, I can't *even* worry about *that*."

GIVE US A KISS

"You have to." I grabbed her by the shoulder. "You have to, Big Annie—I'm fixin' to need a lawyer by breakfast."

"I, oh."

She put her hands to her head.

"Macedonia," Niagra said. "Big Annie? *Big Annie?* Reba and Sonny and them, from when you lived on Blue Goose Commune? They could help. We could run this over to Macedonia—tonight."

"I couldn't."

"I could," Niagra said. Her beauty always did a number on me. I'd miss her. "Doyle's goin' to need the money."

I heard Panda in the hallway, there, working levers, spinning cylinders, rattling boxes of bullets.

Niagra ran her fingertips over my dog-clawed face.

"I love you, Doyle. I ain't talkin' kid stuff, neither."

"You're my dream," I said.

"And you'll have it," she said. "It's just, that, you know, it ain't right what those Dollys did, but they sure did do it."

"Use this one!" Panda shouted. "Or I will!"

"Doyle, honey—you don't have to do what that old man's puttin' you up to. You don't have to—you can just step outside of it, let the law handle it."

She didn't hear it—how could she? There's a kind of devil's music behind it all, the Redmond world, that you can really learn to dance to once you hear it played loud.

I backed away from the girl, the girl I think I loved.

"No," I said. "Who I am, see, won't be that way."

There wasn't much more to say. Panda stood in the doorway, and I knew what he'd be holding. Niagra kissed me.

"We're goin'," she said. "I'll call from Macedonia."

She led Big Annie out the back way, by the hand, and Big Annie forgot to say good-bye. Her feet shuffled like a zombie.

"Smoke," is all she said.

I didn't look at Panda straightaway. I massaged my shoulders, then tipped loose a Lucky and lit up.

"You ain't hittin' me again," I said. "That shit's done."

His cane and his feet made a kind of music as he came at me across the room; thump, shh, thump, shh.

"Use this," he said. "It'll work."

There it was, the Smith and Wesson thirty-eight he'd killed Logan Dolly with. He'd shown his feelings over that shooting by gouging a notch into the handle, the gouge big and prominent.

Such were his sentiments.

I took the pistol, hefted it, checked the cylinder.

He'd loaded it for me.

"More trouble," he said. "That fuckin' sheriff is out front, right now, studying your car mighty close."

I tucked the pistol inside my belt, pulled my shirt over it.

I looked into Panda's blue eyes and saw a mess of stuff in there, stuff that'd be hard to shove back under the lid.

"I'll do what's called for."

28

Closing Time

Sheriff Lilley barked out several harsh comments about me, me and Tararum, delivering these scolds in a hot tone of voice as I crossed the yard, then I put the pistol at his head. I pulled the hammer back to show my level of commitment, and the metallic clicking prompted him to adjust his tone.

"Now, there's nothin' here this serious, Doyle."

"Say you."

"You're makin' this into serious trouble."

I pulled his cuffs from the rear of his belt.

"Assume the position," I said. "I'd rather not hurt butthole kin, not if I can help it."

I had some difficulty with the cuffs, dexterity problems, and I had to shove the gun barrel against the sheriff's head somewhat harder than I wanted to.

"Sorry," I said. "Get your hands back here." He didn't follow orders. His mustache whiffled as he breathed deeply: the idea of fighting me was gaining support in his mind. "Just give me your wrists, Terence, and nothin' tragic has to happen. Not to you, anyhow."

His hands came back slowly, he was a reluctant captive. I slapped the cuffs on, squeezed them shut.

He said, "You started off just guilty of bein' dumb, Doyle, but I can see you won't rest 'til you've took your basic dumb and built it into *dumbest*."

"Whatever."

I led the sheriff by the cuffs, pulled him around to the passenger side of the Volvo. I held the door open for him.

"Get on in—watch your head."

I slammed him in, then went over to the driver's side and slid behind the wheel. The car sounded like a garbage disposal when I turned the engine over. The one headlight shined toward the curb.

"Where're you takin' me?"

"Along for the ride, is all."

"No shit? To where?"

"To get even." I looked at the sheriff there, in the darkness of the car, and he looked back steady. He saw the sincerity in my face. "Smoke got murdered."

He didn't say anything. I thought he might call me a liar, or give a speech about civics, the chain of command, that sort of perfunctory attempt to sway me. But no.

I drove on down Grace Avenue, wrestling the steering wheel as the car was crippled severely, the alignment gone. The headlight illuminated the sidewalks and lawns, but not the road ahead of me.

"That makes me the last," the sheriff said.

I glanced at him and got shocked—he was choking back

some surge of emotion. His cheeks puffed and his lips clinched.

"Huh?"

"Don't you know Smoke'n me schooled together? Shit, son, we both played both ways on the line for the West Table Wuzzahs, lost the district title by a fuckin' field goal. Now, with your brother gone, see, that means I'm the very last man alive from the whole goddamn line." He kicked at the floorboards, tilted his head back in sorrow. "Number seventy-four, he touched a power line. Seventy-eight didn't come back from 'Nam. Sixty-one, shitfire, the doctor said he died of 'acute alcoholism' and he wasn't but thirty-three, thirty-four years old. You wouldn't think you could swallow enough that fast, but he did. One of the backups, Christ, I forgot his number—can you believe that?—he had a bush hog flip on him. Now ol' Smoke, number ninety-one, is out of the lineup, too. That only leaves *me*."

"I'd forgot that was you," I said.

"I haven't," he said. "Seventy-nine for forever."

"You all had a good team."

"Lost by a chickenshit kick—kickin' ain't even football, not really."

I shouldn't have started driving. I didn't know where I was driving to. The car, I think, was close to balking.

"Who killed him?"

"Roy Don Springer."

"And, let me hear you say it—you reckon you're man enough to take *Roy Don Springer*?"

"I've already whipped him once."

"That was you that broke his nose? Good for you,

sonny. But killin' is another deal—and that man is up to it. He's a flat-out bad man—raped Shareena a couple years back, only not with his dick. Used a fireplace poker, ripped her up pitiful. Only instead of pressin' charges, three months later she married him."

"Maybe she'll marry better next time," I said. "She's going to get another chance to, anyhow."

Slager's Liquor Store was shut down for business, but I pulled into the parking lot to think. I really didn't know where to go. Ol' number seventy-nine stared at me and stared at me.

"I don't believe you can take Springer, Doyle," he said after a bit. "So, I'd strongly *advise* you not to go over to The Inca Club, where he most always is this time of night."

White dust from the parking lot swirled in the air. Departing vehicles kicked up billows and plumes of dust, imparting a kind of cloudy look to The Inca Club area. It was near closing time, and only a few pickup trucks and a couple of cars were in the lot.

"I hate to be this way," I said, "but I'm goin' to have to stow you in the trunk."

"The trunk? That's too goddamn much, Doyle."

"That way you couldn't be expected to stop me."

"I ain't gettin in the trunk, son, no—"

I smacked Sheriff Lilley across the knee with the Smith and Wesson. I know that sort of thing hurts.

"This ain't play," I said. "You're gettin' in the trunk."

He fit well enough, even with the spare tire. His expression was pretty sullen as I slapped the lid on him.

I stood outside The Inca Club, thinking about Smoke,

dead in the woods, letting all the voices give pep talks in my head. They told me what was called for.

Forget the modern world, forget what century this is—some stuff runs deeper than that.

I walked toward the door, pistol at my side. I was drawing on a thousand movie scenes, and folktales, Redmond legends, words from mother. *You don't do this to us,* went the refrain in my senses, though, actually, it's been happening to us for fifty or sixty generations, near as I can tell. But the need to say and believe that *you don't do this to us* was chanted in my brain so powerfully that it got my body moving like I knew it to be a bedrock fact.

Shareena showed herself first. She was sitting on the hood of that '57 Chevy shell, holding a bottle of lite beer. I had the pistol in hand. She saw me coming. It seems a few other patrons did as well, since there was sudden movement toward the exit.

"I thought you might be dead," she said.

"Not hardly."

"The night ain't over."

I suppose it *is* a tragedy sometimes, this requirement of being who you are. Who you really are. It was sort of undramatic, though, at least this segment was. Springer came up out of the Chevy shell, his hand inside his trousers, like his pistol had slipped down to his jockey shorts, maybe. That metal thing over his nose, and his blackened eyes, gave him the appearance of a tough-luck sprite, or maybe a gargoyle. He wore khaki pants, and his hand had the fly section really rumpling, like a weasel scurried in there. He had a plaid shirt on, but unbuttoned all the way, and his chest hair seemed luxuriant, salt and pepper in hue, thicker than mine by far. He gave no

Daniel Woodrell

indication of surprise or remorse at seeing me, and didn't seem to fear the pistol I carried.

The jukebox jumped to life, and one of those songs, country songs, where the singer claims whisky has let him down, started to play.

He had it out then. A revolver, snub-nosed.

Shareena laid herself to the floor.

Someone was yelling. Tables and chairs started scooting.

I believe he shot twice, to no effect.

The one round I let off caught him, I thought, high on the chest. He went down, loose as a rug.

I stepped toward him.

"Crawl, you fuckin' worm!" I shouted.

The jukebox plug was jerked. Mr. Wofford stood over there by the wall socket, his hands raised.

"He's past worm-crawlin', Redmond, you doofus. You done snuffed him flat."

I looked closer at the body. The wound seemed to be too centered to kill.

The heart, I guess, isn't exactly where you think it is.

On the way out I snatched a beer off the bar.

I drank it before opening the trunk, I remember that.

Anyhow, I released Sheriff Lilley, apparently, then removed his cuffs. I dropped the pistol.

"I feared for my life," I said. "Take me in."

He busted me in the mouth, cost me a tooth.

"That's for the trunk," he said.

I took the punch okay.

"You kidnap a lawman, Doyle, you've got to expect him to get a li'l red-assed."

29

The Nods

Elrod Chuck, the hottest crime writer in America, who'd never seen fit to blurb any of my novels, came down to Howl County to do a "think piece" on me for *Esquire* magazine. Nickolai Noonan scribbled out a feature for *Vanity Fair,* with excellent photographs. Newspapers and checkout counter tabloids did me proud.

When Smoke visits, we can't keep from marveling at all the attention. The headlines tend to accentuate the hillbilly aspect, HILLBILLY NOVELIST IN HILLBILLY FEUD, that sort of thing. Nickolai Noonan titled his piece "The Pulp He Wrote He Lived," which is kind of windy, I guess, but he's an elegant sentence man. Elrod Chuck stuck with the laconic: "Bloodlines."

Smoke says, "You fuckin' *hothead.* You're famous."

It was, I know now, a sort of murder of errors. Smoke had been carried to the hospital by a lady farmer, one of the Wolfe gals, and was receiving medical attention by the time I threw down on Springer at The Inca Club. He'd been right about that Kansas warrant, too, and used his share from the money garden to iron out the legal wrinkles in his life.

I think I laughed, at least the first time he explained things to me.

Sheriff Lilley treats me like a pal, almost. My agent calls pretty regular, with offers for my next novel or version of the events that led to The Inca Club, et cetera. The sheriff lets me take all of the calls.

The Hyena novels are scheduled to be reprinted in the spring.

Lizbeth, smelling a honey pot of publicity, claims she loves me again.

Most of my time here in the Howl County Jail I spend thinking about golf. Over and over I think about a certain tee-shot at the seventeenth cow pattie, and sometimes I let my shot miss the turd stack, drift wide or fall short, but usually I can't make myself do it, the golf ball flies high and inevitably and irrevocably busts that cow pattie stack to bits.

Uncle Bill sent a postcard from Jeff City saying my room is ready.

Niagra writes long letters expressing her love and re-grets, and details of her assault on the silver screen, from Venice, California.

If I ever get out of prison, I'll be who I always dreamed of being.

My hook found me.